It was 1891. He was wildly attracted to her. He was at her mercy. He was from a completely different world.

"Where are my clothes?"

"Washed, mended, ironed, folded and waiting for you to get better."

Barrett could feel the color rising in his cheeks. "You could at least let me have my Jockeys."

Emma stared at him. "Your what?"

"My . . ." The proper word eluded him for a moment. "My long johns."

She shook her head. "I'm afraid the waistband will aggravate your wound. I don't want to do anything which might start another round of infections."

"What about catching my death of cold?" He pulled his blanket up to his chin, inadvertently exposing his toes in the process.

Emma made a face. She reached below his line of sight and reappeared with a heavier quilt in her hands. "I make it a practice not to let my recovering gunshot patients die of exposure."

"How comforting." He adjusted the quilt for maximum coverage.

"May I ask you a question?" Emma asked.

He nodded.

"What's a Ferrari?"

"A *what?*" he sputtered.

"You kept talking about it when you were delirious. At first, I thought it was a person's name, but you kept talking as if it were more of a something than a someone."

For a moment, he remembered the car, remembered hand-polishing its canary yellow finish, a beloved weekly chore that filled his lonely Sunday mornings. "It's a horse." *Four hundred horses, to be exact.* The image of the vehicle faded, growing unimportant in a world and time where Henry Ford hadn't even built his first car, and where the woman he loved was in front of him.

Praise for A Margin in Time

"Fireworks of the most delightful kind! Laura Hayden has written a charmer!"

—Rosalyn Alsobrook, bestselling author of *Beyond Forever*

LAURA HAYDEN

A MARGIN IN TIME

PINNACLE BOOKS
WINDSOR PUBLISHING CORP.

PINNACLE BOOKS are published by

Windsor Publishing Corp.
850 Third Avenue
New York, NY 10022

The P logo Reg U.S. Pat & TM Off. Pinnacle is a trade-
mark of Windsor Publishing Corp.

First Printing: March, 1995

Printed in the United States of America

To Deb Stover, Pam McCutcheon and
Karen Fox for laughing in all the right places
and always finding a spot in their hearts
(and homes) for the Wandering Minstrel.
To my brother, Mike Beard, who said I should
go into engineering. To Mom and Dad, Kenner
and Ernest, who had faith in me that I could
adapt to any alien atmosphere, be it
underground in a coal mine, on an
Air Force base, above the tree line or above the
Mason-Dixon line.

One

J. Barrett Callan the Fifth looked into the mirror of the executive washroom.

"Ladies and gentlemen of the press, stockholders, fellow employees, it is with a heavy heart—" He stopped. "No, that sounds too theatrical." Barrett flicked a piece of lint from his lapel as he studied his reflection.

"It is with extreme regret that I announce—"

"It is with sadness . . . Damn!" He slammed his fist against the elegant but unfortunately hard marble sink, wincing as he recoiled in pain.

Barrett examined the new nick in the garnet-colored stone of his class ring. *Bright move, Boy Genius. Break your hand right before a press conference. That would certainly amuse the vultures out there who are ready to pick your bones anyway.*

He glared at himself, then straightened his tie. Lifting his chin, he examined the skin along his jaw line. A strong jaw, he thought. One which exuded strength and character.

But did it impart a sense of honesty? If it didn't, his days of relative freedom were numbered.

I trusted Crawford and now I'm going to pay for that bastard's greed with my career. His stomach soured again. *Or with my freedom . . .*

He glanced at his watch.

Five minutes until High Noon.

Five minutes!

A sudden flare of pain fired his stomach. *Five minutes until I face the firing squad.* The acid churned, sending him to paw through the cabinet by the mirror, where he discovered a near-empty bottle of antacid. Two lone tablets tumbled out into the palm of his hand.

"The beginning of the end and I'm almost out of Rolaids." He sneered at himself as he tossed the tablets in his mouth. "How do you spell relief? B-A-N-K-R-U-P-T-C-Y," he mumbled around the Rolaids, "That's how."

"No, R-E-L-I-E-F," echoed a solemn voice.

Barrett pivoted, searching for the source of the familiar-sounding voice. "Who said that?"

Only an eerie silence answered him.

He drew a deep breath, spun and, leaning closer to the mirror, stared into the pained eyes. "You're starting to lose it, Mister Callan," he said. "Now that the world around you is falling apart, I suppose it's no wonder you're hearing voices. Maybe it's time to check into a twelve-step padded room program."

"What th' hell you talking about, boy?"

Barrett grabbed the sink with both hands to steady himself. He knew that voice all too well; he'd spoken the words.

This time, his mirrored mouth didn't even move as he whispered, "Oh, Good Lord . . . I'm schizophrenic, and I don't even know it!"

The image looked puzzled. "What's a schiza-schizo-free-nic? Some sort of foreigner?" The mirrored Barrett ran a hand along his chin. "I think we could use a shave. Feels a mite rough to me."

Barrett gaped at the reflection which seemed to have a mind of its own. After batting on the hot water tap, Barrett pawed blindly through the drawer for the can of shaving cream.

Don't think about him. Just shave. It's nothing but the sushi I had for lunch talking back to me. Barrett shook the can violently. *Just ignore the face in the mir—*

"You got a straight razor in this fancy outhouse?" The image asked, making a great show of looking around the executive rest room. "Don't tell me you're one of those dandies who has to have a barber perform the duty. Can't abide barbers, 'specially the ones where I come from."

"Who are . . . what are . . ."

A hand extended from the mirror, which Barrett instinctively reached for until self-preservation saved him.

"Johnny Callaghan's the name."

"C-Calla—"

The image grinned. "Your great-great-grandfather, boy."

Barrett's bum knee threatened to collapse as his stomach lurched again. *If they hear me talking to myself, the press will have me signed, sealed, and committed inside the hour!* He glared at the smirking face in the mirror. Sudden suspicions formed a protective barrier around him. "Now wait a second . . . you said your name was Callaghan."

"Yep."

"B-but my name's . . ." In the light of a momentary confusion, Barrett forgot.

"Callan." The image spoke the name with obvious contempt. "I'll be damned if I know why your great-grandfather decided he had to change it. What's wrong with the name 'Callaghan,' I ask you?"

"C-Calla—"

"And that portrait of me! The one hanging over your desk. I'll have you know, boy, that I owned only one fancy suit in my life. Got married in it, got buried in it and I never looked like the . . . the old coot that Johnny Junior had me painted up as. Hell . . . I died when he was only ten and

I was only forty-two, at that. I don't know who that old so-and-so in the portrait is, but it sure as hell ain't me!"

"Y-you died . . . ?" His throat tightened, choking off the words.

"Hell, yeah, I died. If I hadn't, I'd be . . ." The image stopped and screwed up his face in calculation. "Lessee . . . I'd be a hundred and thirty-three years old." He began to laugh. "And a durn sight uglier than I am now!"

Suddenly, Barrett feared the last vestiges of his sanity were pouring onto the floor. No . . . it was the water which had filled the sink and now cascaded over the edges of the cabinet to soak his Italian leather loafers.

A cloud of steam rose to fog the mirror. The image, who called himself . . . itself . . . himself Johnny Callaghan, calmly wiped the glass with his hand, clearing a clean spot. "Son, you're makin' a big mess . . ." He pointed to the river of water.

Barrett obediently turned off the tap, burning his hand in the process. He released a string of oaths that only seemed to amuse his mirrored image.

"Whew!" Johnny gave him a crooked grin. "For a while there, I thought you was as sissified as your clothes. Does me good to hear you swear up a storm, son. Makes you sound like a man . . ." He paused to give Barrett a scathing once-over. "Even if you don't much look like one."

Barrett stiffened. What criteria did a man use to select the suit which best reflected his news of failure? What was the proper fashion for a man about to announce the impending demise of a hundred-year-old business? *Dress For Success* didn't include a chapter on dressing for failure.

"You make us look like a two-bit dandy," Johnny continued, pulling at the red power tie knotted in a perfect double Windsor.

"Us . . ." It was no longer a question.

Johnny shifted his hand up his chin. "Spooky, ain't it? This wasn't even my face first. Always seems to skip a generation. My Aunt Phoebe always said I looked a lot like my grandpaw. Nothing like my daddy at all. Johnny Junior got his looks from his maw's side of the family. But your grandfather, John the Third, looked like this, and you do, too. Of course, you don't act a whit like 'em."

"What do you mean?"

"You're headed out that door to tell those people you lost all their money." Flat contempt colored the words, making Barrett's stomach turn again.

"I didn't lose their money. There were downturns in the economy I couldn't anticipate, and—"

"Boy . . . don't make excuses. You had

their money. Now you don't." The face in the mirror hardened. "Fancy explanations ain't gonna keep them from puttin' a rope around your neck and findin' a tall tree."

Barrett couldn't help but laugh. "A hanging? Thank God, no." He paused, imagining himself swinging by the red silk tie. "They don't do that anymore," he mumbled half to himself.

The image scratched his head, then stared at the class ring on Barrett's hand. "Son, men of your day have got it damned easy. Fancy clothes, flashy jewelry . . ." He turned his hands over and stared down at his palms with a grimace. "And soft hands. These look as if they've never done a lick of hard work."

Barrett adjusted his coat, suddenly self-conscious of his manicure. "I don't make a living with my hands."

Johnny caught him a steel-trap stare. "Don't do much of one with your head, either." He released a sigh. "Son, you're in for a mess of trouble when you step out there. Maybe people of your day and age don't go for a good lynchin', but they're looking for blood. Your blood."

Sagging against the wet counter, Barrett acknowledged his fears for the first time. There were disgruntled stockholders outside as well as reporters, banking officials and, rumor had it, federal officers bearing warrants. He knew he hadn't done anything illegal, other than be incredibly naive and put his trust where it didn't belong. How could he explain to any of them that the company's trust funds were somewhere on the beaches of Rio with the company's rogue vice president?

"What do I do?" he whispered to himself. He looked in the mirror and addressed the image there, forgetting it wasn't J. Barrett Callan. Him. "What do I do?" he repeated.

"Escape."

It was a sweet word, one promising release from the choke hold of responsibility. It was also a forbidden word. Callans didn't shirk their obligations—no matter how painful. Protection of his family's reputation and name had been drilled into him practically from the womb.

"Callans don't run," he stated flatly.

"But you ain't a Callan. You're a Call-a*ghan*. You're John Barrett Callaghan the Fifth." He smiled slightly. "How would you like to escape from the pack of hungry animals waiting to feed on your carcass?"

"How?"

Johnny crossed his arms and his smile widened. "Trade places with me."

Barrett stared at his reflection, at Johnny's grin. It'd been too long since he'd seen a smile on his own face. There had been precious little to amuse him since the bankruptcy became the final and only solution. "Trade places?" he managed around his disbelief. "Now I *know* I'm insane."

The man in the mirror grew solemn. "It would be a solution to both our problems, son. The problems here in the future could be avoided in the past."

"W-what do you mean?"

Johnny's gaze sharpened. "You're not facing bankruptcy because you trusted a scoundrel. If you'd gotten your hands on those parcels of land at the base of the mountain, you'd never even have thought about reinvesting the retirement funds, right? If you owned that tract, the mining operation could still continue."

Barrett thought about the tangled mess of paperwork which, had he been able to unravel it, might have meant the survival of the hundred-year-old family business. He took a deep breath before speaking. "Y-yes, I failed. Failed everybody. I tried . . . I really tried, but I couldn't get the deed situation cleared up in order to buy the land."

Johnny reached into the sharp-looking suit and pulled out a yellowed piece of paper. "You mean this?" He held it up, allowing Barrett to read the old-styled print.

Barrett smacked his hand against the mirror, forgetting he was talking to an image of his own unchecked, perhaps feverish imagination. He wiped away an irritating bead of sweat from his upper lip. "Where'd you get that?"

"The townspeople of Margin, Colorado gave me the deed to hold in good faith for 'em."

Margin? Barrett cleared his throat. "That's nothing but an old ghost town near the mine shaft. No one lives there now."

"They did back in my time. In the 1890s, it was a nice little town. A good place to live and to work. The Daisy Lee wasn't the richest mine in the area, but it was keeping our town afloat. Until . . ." Johnny's voice trailed off.

Barrett knew the history of the lately lamented town of Margin; it had been a lore handed down from father to son. "Until the mine collapsed," he repeated verbatim. "And the people sold their land to the 'Continental Silver and Copper Consortium.' "

Johnny looked shocked. "Hell, no! Until Thornwald blew up the mine and tricked the townspeople into selling."

This revelation destroyed years of stories Barrett had learned at his father's knee about the virtuous Thornwald who had become a partner with the original J.B. Callan. "Tricked? But I always thought . . ."

Johnny flushed. "What you heard was a pack of lies Johnny Junior used to cover up my stupidity. I trusted that weasel Thornwald and he turned on me, cheating my friends out of their just due. I've been stuck here on Earth, watching myself make the same damn mistakes over and over again. I've been given three chances to change the past—with my son, my grandson, and my great-grandson. Each time I've failed. You're my last chance, boy."

"Last chance . . . how?"

"None of the men in the family were willing to trade places with me. I came to each of them during their thirty-second year and asked them to trade. But each of 'em had families, a successful business to run. But you . . ." A sad smile curled his lips. "You've got nothing. No woman—"

"Hold it. What about . . ." Barrett searched for a name, compelled to defend his empty love life with a lie, if necessary. "What about Angela?"

As soon as he spoke her name, Barrett felt a chill across his skin. His secretary's icy blue eyes could freeze a man at twenty paces. And despite his best efforts, the Deep Freeze Queen hadn't thawed one degree in the three years she'd worked as his personal assistant.

Johnny shook his head. "Like I said, no women, no children, no future except one probably behind bars. And you're not likely to give me a fourth chance by becoming a father while stuck in prison." Johnny pointed past Barrett's shoulder toward the door. "There's a man out there, in the front row, with a warrant for your arrest. If you trade places in time with me, you can solve your problems before they ever happen. The townspeople keep the Daisy Lee mine, and the business survives. You never face bankruptcy. You never go to jail. Hell . . . you might even become a daddy one day."

A catch. There has to be a catch. "What about you? What do *you* get out of this?"

Johnny shrugged. "I get to leave this place and go to my reward. Heaven or hell . . . either would be a plain sight better than remaining here. In the In-Between."

Barrett stared at the hot water burn on his hand.

Reality was painful. It was supposed to be.

And in his case, reality would mean federal warrants.

Expensive lawyers.

A couple of overturned appeals.

And probably a stint in a country club prison for high-class embezzlers. But a prison nonetheless.

"It's not that bad, boy."

Barrett looked up into Johnny's smile. His smile. Johnny's smile. "What? Can you read my thoughts, too?" *Maybe it's time to make reservations at the Betty Ford clinic. A nice room in the corner with a view. And rubber walls.*

Johnny screwed up his face. "You're thinking about a woman. Some lady named Betty who runs . . . a hotel? Is she important to you? A girlfriend or somethin'?"

Barrett managed to shake his head before he began to choke on the irony of Johnny's misconception. "No, not quite." He stared at the man he was beginning to believe *was* his great-great-grandfather. "How do we do it, Johnny? How do I save everything?"

"You convince the people to keep their land." Johnny crossed his arms. "Tell 'em about the copper vein that's alongside the silver strike."

Barrett shrugged. "If it's that simple, why don't you tell them?"

"I wish it'd be as easy as that. When I go back, I can't remember anything about the future." Johnny's face darkened. "I keep makin' the same damn mistakes over and over again. Only you can save me from this hell of In-Between." He stared at Barrett, his face softening. "Only you . . . son."

Barrett glanced over his shoulder at the bathroom door, then turned back to face Johnny, drawing a deep breath. "How do we do it? Trade places, that is?"

Johnny smiled. "Take my hand."

"But how . . ."

"Don't ask questions, boy. Just do it!"

The mirror quivered, rippling like a stone-struck pond of liquid silver. A hand emerged, mirroring to his own. The twin garnet stones in the matching class rings reflected the overhead light. When he clasped the proffered hand, he felt the lightest spark of contact, a shiver of electricity between them.

"Pull!" his great-great-grandfather commanded.

Barrett pulled.

His fingers curled around the ivory inlaid handle of the straight razor. As he held the blade to his cheek, he looked into the mirror, seeing a tired face covered with a splotchy coat of shaving cream. For a moment, he didn't recognize the image, then his stomach sent up a mighty protest. Barrett dropped the razor in the basin of water.

"Holy shit!"

"That's the first thing I said when I saw you, boy." The image in the mirror, Johnny Callaghan, winked. "You be damned careful with that razor. That's *my* face you'll be carvin' up."

Barrett tore his gaze from the image and looked around the bare room. A thin bed, a small bookcase, a desk, an oil lamp. A far cry from the luxuries of the executive washroom of Callan Industries.

"But . . ."

"Don't worry, boy. I'll see what I can do to help on this end. Just make damn sure the townspeople don't cave in to Thornwald and that blasted mining company." Johnny shook his head as if trying to displace unpleasant memories. His eyes narrowed. "One more thing." His hand extended through the mirror surface and he held out a couple sheets of crumpled paper.

Barrett stared at them for a moment before reaching out. "What's this?"

"Information about the people around you." Johnny shook a finger at him. "Now you make sure you read that before you step one foot outside that door. You'll make a damn fool out of yourself—out of me—if you don't know the people and the places you're supposed to know."

"But . . ."

Johnny pointed again, this time at Barrett's right hand. "Don't forget to take off that thing, boy."

Barrett glanced down, spotting the class ring which glimmered in the soft light. A tremor coursed through his hand, betraying his frayed nerves. "My ring. Of . . . of course." As he struggled to pull the ring over his knuckle, he caught sight of the dingy long johns he wore instead of his usual briefs. He grimaced, then allowed himself a brief internal smile. What would Johnny do when he discovered he had on a pair of red boxer shorts emblazoned with hearts that glowed in the dark?

"Good luck, Barrett. Of course, you're Johnny, now. Johnny Callaghan." The smiling image started to fade. "Ya gotta act like me, look like me—"

"But wait!' Barrett called out. "What do you do? What's your profession?"

Johnny gave him a soap-flecked grin. "Didn't I tell you? I'm the sheriff. My gun's hanging on the bedpost. Now don't you even think about leaving this room without wearing that holster. And don't forget the badge. You have a reputation to maintain. Mine!"

The image faded away before Barrett could protest, leaving nothing but the room reflected in the mirror. *Like a vampire . . . no reflection*. He saw the clothes laid across the bed and turned to gape at the shiny badge pinned to the shirt. When he turned back, he was startled by the image in the mirror.

"Johnny!"

He and the image spoke simultaneously.

It was his reflection.

Barrett looked down at the razor sitting in the bottom of the water basin, then glanced at his face. With an unsteady hand, he fished out the razor, then held it to his cheek.

TWO

Another one?

Barrett stemmed the flow of blood with his finger, knowing there would be no convenient roll of toilet paper to stick on his shaving cuts. Pressing the thin towel to his self-inflicted wounds, he eyed Johnny's clothes.

Not what we'd call designer threads . . .

After he dressed, Barrett discovered the papers his great-great-grandfather had given him included a list and descriptions of townspeople as well as a crude map of Margin. After studying the paper for so long that the spiky, handwritten words swam together, Barrett gingerly strapped on the holster and gun. He found the back exit which took him out of the boarding house via an exterior staircase and down to the dusty streets of Margin. According to the map, the sheriff's office was across the street.

He surveyed the sporadic traffic, mostly pedestrian, a few horses and wagons. *Oh God . . . let me get to the office before anybody—*

"Mornin', Sheriff." The man paused on the wooden sidewalk and shifted the barrel he had balanced across one shoulder.

Barrett offered a half smile. "Mornin' . . . Silas." Thank God, Johnny had identified Silas Brainard, town grocer, by his terminally soiled apron and shock of bright red hair.

The grocer eyed him for one uncomfortable second, then the man began to chuckle. "Looks like Lemuel's fingers were shaking when he did your morning shave, Johnny. I thought you said you'd never let that butcher put a razor to you again."

Barrett felt the flush start at the collar of Johnny's shirt and head up. In his hands, the straight razor had become a lethal weapon. He'd come close to slitting his throat while performing a simple task men used to do every morning in the old days. He tried to cover his embarrassment by giving Silas a Western movie tough-guy smirk.

The grocer merely shot Barrett an odd glance and muttered, "Must have been a late night . . . eh, Johnny?" The man wandered away, shaking his flaming hair.

Swallowing hard, Barrett stepped into the dirt street. A thin layer of dust quickly covered his scuffed boots as he made a beeline for the office. He sent up a fervent prayer, his first in some time, hoping to avoid meeting anybody else along the way. Graced by whatever or whoever was in cosmic charge,

Barrett managed to reach the door. He ducked in the office, pausing to take a deep breath and add a corollary of thanks to his prayer. *So far so—*

"Morning, Sheriff."

Barrett jumped.

The voice came from the back of the room. "I've swept out the cells, picked up your mail, cleaned up Harvey, and . . ." A young boy stepped out of the shadows and into the muddy puddle of light filtering through the dirty windows. " . . . I was wondering if . . . if you might not mind if I . . ." The boy's voice trailed off as he paid an inordinate amount of attention to the black hat he gripped.

"If I would what?" *I'll give you anything if you'd just get out of here and let me try to figure out what's going on.*

"If you wouldn't mind advancin' me a nickel on my next pay? It's my sister's birthday tomorrow . . ."

Barrett remembered Johnny's warning about his young assistant whose "tongue is hinged in the middle and wags both ways." Barrett searched his memory for the kid's name.

The boy continued. ". . . and I was hoping I could buy her a new cloth rose for her Sunday hat. She's had her eye on one at Mr. Brainard's store for a while and I thought—"

Barrett reached into his pocket and pulled

out a coin, barely glancing at it before he flipped it to the boy. "Here . . . son. Buy her that rose and tell her happy birthday for me."

The young boy, whose name Barrett couldn't remember, stared at the disk in his hand. His voice was low and hushed. "A silver dollar? A whole silver dollar? Sheriff . . . I . . . I don't know what . . ." Suddenly the young boy hurled himself at Barrett, gave him an awkward hug, then stepped back. "Thanks, Johnny . . . er, Sheriff Callaghan. Emma will be so surprised!" The kid ran out the door, slamming it hard enough to rattle the windows.

"That was stupid."

Barrett jumped for the second time.

The voice continued from the darkness. "When his sister finds out what you did, she's gonna come looking for you with a ruler in her hand."

"A ruler?"

"Schoolmarms have a thing about whacking people on the hand with their rulers." There was a hint of laughter in the gruff voice.

Barrett moved closer to the barred cell, watching the man rise from the cot. "Why should the lady be angry? All he wants to do is buy her a present. It was only a buck."

"Only a buck? Try a month's salary. I suspect Miz Emma Nolan is counting on Ford's pay to help build a nest egg for winter, not to buy fancy frills she'll never use. Teachers don't make much in this century, either."

Barrett had already half-formulated his next rebuttal when the significance of the man's words hit him. *In* this *century?* He swallowed his retort and moved closer to inspect the grizzled face. "What do you mean . . . this century?"

The man smiled, showing a straight set of teeth beneath the grimy beard. "Johnny said you might have a bit of trouble *rectifyin'* yourself to this era. Judging by the cuts on your face, he was right."

Barrett ran a self-conscious hand over the places on his cheek that still stung from his own brand of butchery. "How do you . . . I mean . . ."

The man took an ornate pocket watch from his wrinkled vest. A soft, tinkling melody echoed through the cell. "How do you think a man from the nineteenth century learns about time travel? I know Johnny's never read any H.G. Wells. So it has to be from me." The man passed one hand over the ornate clock face and the fancy numbers disappeared, replaced by a black circle. He reached into the blackness with two fingers and pulled out a cigar.

"Ahh . . . Cuban, my favorite."

Barrett couldn't stop his mouth from dropping open.

The man reached in again and produced a butane lighter, then lit the cigar. He grinned around the cigar clenched firmly between his perfect teeth. "I'd reach in and find you an electric razor, but it doesn't work that way. It can only replicate for me."

He shoved the lighter back into the watch's dark void which violated, in Barrett's opinion, at least three basic laws of physics and nature.

It's a dream. Angela's going to knock on the bathroom door and discover me curled in a fetal position on the floor. Then the men in white are going to cart me off, a useless piece of catatonic yuppie flesh.

"You okay?"

Barrett shook himself back to the present . . . the past. "What is that thing?" He pointed at the pocket watch.

"A combination portal locator, scan unit, temporal stabilizer and miniature replicator. I'm a traveler, too."

"A t-traveler?"

"Time traveler. The name's Kirk, Harvey J. Kirk, and please . . ." He held up a hand in caution. "Before you make any remarks . . . yes, the 'J' does stand for James, but I won't stand any cracks about "Star Trek." I've heard every joke in the universe about the name. I think my parents had a real perverted sense of humor." He fiddled with a button on the portal watch. "Everybody calls me Harvey."

Barrett thumbed over his shoulder. "The Harvey that Johnny was talking about? The one in—"

The man nodded. "The one in Johnny's notes. But he didn't tell you why he said to make sure you locked me up every Saturday night, did he?"

Barrett thought back about the cryptic comments in the letter. He'd assumed this Harvey character was the town drunk, like Otis in the old "Andy Griffith Show." An affable, harmless drunk who tanked up every Saturday night, slept it off all day Sunday, and was always turned loose on Monday mornings.

Kirk continued. "You could have knocked me over with the feather from a Rygellian soaring bird when I stepped through the portal field and found myself in this jail cell somewhere in the Colorado Rockies during the 1890s, the heyday of the silver mines. Whoever coordinated the door misjudged the specs by at least forty feet. The portal was supposed to appear in some back alley, not the solid stone wall of a jail cell.

"The c-cell," Barrett stuttered.

"Sure . . ." Harvey Kirk turned and made a show of leaning his elbow against the wall. "See?"

He disappeared. Only a puff of cigar smoke drifted from the once solid wall.

Barrett grabbed the cold iron bars. "Kirk!"

The man leaned back, returning from whatever void had swallowed him. "You can see why I had to take Johnny into my confidence. It was either pose as a drunk or not have a chance to visit this time period at all."

Barrett reached out blindly behind him and found the desk chair. Sitting with an ungraceful lurch, he merely stared at the man. "This time period," he repeated in a leaden voice.

Harvey sat down as well and tugged on his boots. "Sure. What better way can a historian study and really get to understand a time other than visit it himself?" His watch gave an odd chirp and he glanced down at it. "Uh . . . oh. Company coming. Think I'll lie down." He dropped to the cot, stuffed his watch in his vest, and in seconds appeared to be an old reprobate sleeping off a night on the town.

Barrett heard a sharp rap, sounding all the world like a thick ruler against the wooden door.

"Sheriff Callaghan? I need to speak with you. Now!" The feminine voice carried across the threshold in strident waves.

He stared at Harvey who cracked open one eye, shook his head, and feigned sleep again.

Barrett's voice wavered. "Uh . . . come in."

She wore gray.

It was the first thing he noticed about her. She reminded him of the quintessential grammar school teacher, commanding instant attention whenever she entered a room. The serious gray cloak screamed *Respect!*, but an undone top button betrayed a flash of soft lavender.

"Sheriff Callaghan, I cannot believe you are willing to corrupt a child's work ethic by allowing Ford to squander away his pay on useless gewgaws!" She held out her hand to reveal the silver dollar resting in the center of her palm.

"I . . . uh—" The words choked in his throat as he glanced up from the coin to her face. Every trite statement he'd ever heard about *beauty* trooped through his mind.

Skin-deep.

In the eye of the beholder.

Barrett swallowed hard.

She continued to glare at him with obvious contempt. "As Ford's sole guardian, it is my duty to try to instill in him a sense of responsibility. After our parents died, it became my duty to teach him how to ration the good fortune of one season to cover the shortages of the next. Your unusual generosity only serves to confuse my brother, and I wish you would refrain from any further bursts of magnanimity." She slammed the coin on his desk.

"M-magnanimity?" Barrett was pleased to have worked a single word in edgewise, much less one of five syllables.

"Magnanimity," she repeated. "It's a noun, and it means—"

"I know what it means to be magnanimous," he offered, taking great satisfaction as she registered shock. He leaned forward and added in raised-eyebrow confidence, "It's an adjective meaning to be generous or noble, or in some cases, forgiving. You might try experiencing a burst of magnanimity yourself on occasions. Starting with me."

She gaped at him.

He continued. "I'll admit I overpaid Ford. It was an accident." Old protective instincts rushed to the surface, the smooth talker reappearing from the depths of a bankruptcy-inspired depression. "When I reached into my pocket, I didn't realize I'd pulled out the silver dollar until it was too late. There was nothing I could do. Anyway . . ." He glanced at Harvey for reassurance, but the Benedict Arnold did nothing but roll over on the cot and release a rattling snore. "Uh . . . anyway, Ford does a good job around here. Why shouldn't he get a reward every now and then?" Barrett fished in his pocket and pulled out a nickel. He reached over and snagged her wrist, trying to ignore the momentary flash of discomfort as he pressed the coin into her palm.

"But . . ." Her voice trailed off as she glanced up.

He expected her eyes to be gray to match her cloak. Schoolmarm gray, with chalky streaks like a smeared blackboard. But when her hesitant glance met his, he discovered her eyes were blue. A glorious good-morning blue like the columbines which used to grow around his grandmother's mail box.

For a moment he smiled, remembering the indescribable feeling of belonging when he thought about his grandmother's house. Then the feeling of warmth shifted. For a split second, the woman in front of him shared his smile, became a part of his sense of acceptance. Barrett realized he still had her hand caught in the circle of his fingers. He released her quickly, watching the confused glimmer of a smile fade from her eyes.

"Give this to Ford . . . please. Tell him it's a bonus, not an advance."

She opened her mouth to argue but evidently thought better of it. She closed her fingers around the coin. "I suppose . . . I suppose it would be all right." A look of determination returned to her face, erasing the softness which had flooded it moments before. "As long as you don't make a habit of this extreme generosity."

Barrett knew Harvey was right; she probably wanted to take her ruler and give his recalcitrant schoolboy-like wrist a slap. He shrugged. "Yes, ma'am." He watched her as she pivoted and headed out. Once the door rattled shut, Barrett remembered to breathe again, starting with a raspy gasp.

"Congratulations." Harvey smiled as he rose from his cot.

"Why?"

"I don't think I've ever seen anybody left standing when Hurricane Emma swept through a room."

Barrett thought of brilliant sky blue eyes hidden beneath a swirl of storm-gray clouds. "Her name's . . . Emma?"

Harvey pushed the cell door open. "Yep. Emma Nolan. Interesting story. Her old man was a doctor down in Tennessee. The town raised the money to bring the good doctor and his family here to start a new practice in Margin. Only trouble was, Dr. Nolan died during the trip here. Emma felt a sense of responsibility to the town for advancing her family's train fare, so she offered to work off the debt as a schoolteacher. She certainly acts like she's made of stern stuff, but I understand all the kids love her."

Barrett continued to stare at the faded curtains, which still swung from the motion of the door. "Kids . . ." he muttered. "Yeah, kids have a way of seeing things adults don't."

Harvey's laughter filled the small office, bouncing off the stone walls. "This is going to be fun! Educational, even. Johnny never gave that woman the time of day before, but I saw the looks she gave him behind his back."

"Burying mental daggers in his back?" Barrett offered.

"Hardly. More like a hungry child watching someone eat. She's the spinster schoolmarm now, not likely to capture a man."

"Spinster? She couldn't be more than thirty!"

"Twenty-six."

"Twenty-six," Barrett repeated flatly. "Over the hill and coasting toward oblivion."

"In this era, it is."

"This era . . ." Barrett spun to face the man. "I don't know anything about this time period. I was a lousy history student. The only things left of Margin in my world are some fallen timbers and a couple of blackened chimneys." He smiled, remembering his childhood. "I used to play army with my friends in the ruins near the mine. I never thought about who might have lived there . . ."

"*Lives* here, you mean. You live here now, too. In fact, you're stuck here until you change history."

"Stuck here?"

Harvey shrugged. "Until you do whatever

it is you're supposed to do to affect your future." He took a long draw on his cigar and released a lazy cloud of smoke in Barrett's direction. "You do remember what you're supposed to do, don't you?"

"The mine." Barrett ambled across the room and shifted the tattered curtain out of the way. "I'm here to make sure the townspeople don't sell out to Thornwald." He squinted through the murky glass.

"He blows up the mine, you know."

Barrett felt his heart take an extra thundering beat. "Then you *do* know the future!" He pivoted. "Do I succeed? Do I keep the people from losing their land to that crook?"

Harvey stared at him for a long moment, then slowly shook his head, disappointment coloring his features.

"I don't save the mine?" Barrett's stomach began to churn.

"No, that's not it. We've got a lot of work to do to convince these people you're Sheriff Johnny Callaghan." The man pointed over his shoulder in the opposite direction and released a heavy sigh. "The mine's that way."

"Okay . . . so I have a lousy sense of direction." Barrett found a cracked mirror beside the door and shifted to view his reflection. For a brief second, he expected the image to speak back to him. "At least I look like Johnny, don't I?"

"Hell, you're the spitting image of him! It's damn spooky. But spitting isn't enough. You've got to sound like him, walk like him, shoot like him—"

"Shoot?" Suddenly the gun strapped to Barrett's side weighed twenty pounds heavier.

Harvey gave him a sour look. "You've never shot a gun before, have you?"

"Uh . . . no."

"How about horses . . . do you ride?"

Barrett's stomach performed a three and a half in a pike position. "English saddle. Twice."

Harvey stared at him. "And it's obvious you've never used a straight razor in your life." He winced sympathetically as Barrett fingered one of many cuts on his face which still stung. "But . . . not to worry. Lemuel, the local barber can't do much better. Lessee, you can't ride, you can't shoot, you can't—"

"Sheriff! Sheriff Callaghan!" Ford Nolan burst through the door, looking as if he had just run a marathon. "Trouble down at the Crystal Plume. Hurry!"

Barrett felt his heart wedge in his throat. "What kind of trouble?"

The boy shot him a puzzled look. "Same as usual, Sheriff."

So much for stalling tactics. Barrett stared over the boy's head at Harvey and sent out a silent plea for help.

Harvey rolled his eyes. "You go ahead, Ford. Sheriff'll be there in a minute."

Ford hesitated for a beat, bouncing his amazed look from Barrett to Harvey and back again. "Y-yes sir." He sped through the door, the windows rattling in his wake.

"I . . . I didn't know what to say," Barrett offered. "What do I do now?"

Harvey pushed open the unlocked cell door and moved quickly to the glass-front cabinet by the desk. He opened the door, reached in, and pulled out a shotgun. "You'll need this." He shoved the weapon into Barrett's sweaty hand, then rummaged through the desk drawer. "And these." He thrust a couple of shotgun shells at Barrett.

"What's this?"

"Ammunition, you idiot."

"But it's—"

"Shut up. Just load 'em . . ." Harvey muttered an expletive under his breath as he observed Barrett's first attempt ever to load a shotgun. "Have to do everything myself . . . Here!" He grabbed the gun, broke it open, loaded it, and rammed it back into Barrett's hesitant grasp. "Two blocks down and on the right. If she doesn't stop, shoot her."

"S-shoot . . . *her?*"

Harvey nodded. "Matilda," he offered as if it were all the explanation Barrett needed.

Barrett stumbled out into the daylight, amazed how the dirty windows had muted

the bright sunshine. He trotted down the
street, gun in hand, and spotted the group
of people gathered on the sidewalk ahead.
Shouldering his way through the crowd, he
glanced up at the intricate stained glass sign
bearing a peacock.

The Crystal Plume.

He could hear hideous noises coming
from the bar, terrifying bellows that raised
the hackles on the back of his neck. Choking
back his rising panic, Barrett stepped into
the bar, shotgun lifted and nerves poised on
the brink of splintering.

As he stared blankly at the scene in front
of him, the gun barrel lowered and his
mouth dropped open.

Two females.

One stretched out in motionless, poised
splendor, on a bed of feathers. She wore a
pleasant, painted expression, a gilded frame
and absolutely nothing else.

The second female wore fur.

In fact she was covered in fur, and the
noises emanating from her would wake the
dead. It was a song of love, Barrett decided
later, of unrequited love that Matilda
bawled, hoping to raise the dead.

And the man of her dreams was indeed
deceased.

Dead, stuffed, and mounted on the wall.

The female moose pawed the floor, leaving long fresh streaks in the wooden planks.

She lifted her head and bellowed once more. The object of her obvious affection, a magnificent stuffed moose head, remained silent.

"Oh my God . . ."

"Well just don't stand there, Johnny." The bartender waved a broom toward the lovesick moose. "Do something!"

Barrett gulped.

"Shoot her!"

Doesn't this town have an animal control officer or something?

"Sheriff, hurry . . . Matilda's ruining the floor!"

Barrett lifted the shotgun, which suddenly weighed a ton, and aimed in the general direction of the moose's wide rear. He had a sudden vision of Chuck Connors, stalking through the streets of whatever Western television town he lived in, guns ablazing.

Step. Fire. Step. Fire.

Dammit. That was "The Rifleman," not the "Shotgun Man." How the heck do I fire this thing?

He fumbled with the trigger and the shotgun roared.

The moose's love song turned sour, and she reared, screaming one more impassioned cry to her intended mate before she ran through the clear path the townspeople thoughtfully made for her. As she passed the crowd of onlookers in her retreat and headed outside, the rock salt embedded in her hide glistened in the sunlight.

The bartender walked around the end of the polished counter and stared glumly at the fresh grooves in the floor. "Damn she-moose! When ya going to use some real buckshot on her, Johnny?"

"Aw c'mon, Earl." Silas Brainard slapped the man on the back. "Her hide's so thick that buckshot'd just get her mad and then she'd really tear up the place. Or leave more than just scratches on your floor." The red-headed grocer pointed to the moose head. "If you'd just take that silly thing down, Matilda wouldn't keep coming in here during mating season."

"It ain't mating season," the bartender grumbled. "And anyways, why should I destroy the ambivalence of this place just because of some stupid she-moose?"

"Ambiance. Not ambivalence." Barrett spoke without thinking, then clamped his mouth shut. He handled the gun uneasily, not knowing how to carry the weapon now that it wasn't needed. Red-faced, he muttered something completely incoherent even to himself, pivoted, and headed out. As he pushed his way through the swinging doors, he felt the uneasy sensation of being caught in the steely net of a blue-eyed stare. When he looked up, Emma Nolan didn't turn away, maintaining an uncomfortable eye contact with him.

First "magnanimous." Then, "ambivalence."

He was slipping, digging his own grave with a four-syllabled shovel. And Emma Nolan was watching him do it.

Barrett winced, remembering how the company's bankruptcy had been born in the womb of vocabulary. A judicious use of words and phrases had hidden the theft of the trust funds, providing a paper camouflage which protected the guilty and threw blame on the innocent.

Not again. Not to Mrs. Callan's fair-haired boy—Whoa!

Barrett deftly sidestepped a moose-patty which the animal had so thoughtfully deposited outside rather than in the bar.

I'm not taking any crap from anybody . . . or anything.

Three

"I just ironed that shirt, Ford." Emma watched her brother shove the folded garment under his arm while keeping his rapt attention on the magazine in his hands.

"Uh-huh . . ."

"Ford."

"Ford!"

"Ford!"

He looked up, startled. "What?"

"Put the shirt up before you wrinkle it . . . please."

Ford released a theatrical sigh and stomped down the hallway to his room. Moments later, he returned, sans shirt and with his nose buried again in his magazine.

"Did you stack the wood like I asked you to?"

He stood in the middle of the room. "Uh-huh . . ."

"Did you fill the cistern?"

"Hmmm . . . uh-huh." He flipped a page.

"Did you climb to the roof, stick feathers

in your ears, and try to flap your way to San Francisco?"

Ford didn't even look up. "Like an eagle, Sis. Like an eagle."

She graced his bowed head with an indulgent smile. "That's a good story, isn't it?"

Drawing a deep breath, he pulled a narrow piece of leather from his pocket and inserted it between the pages before closing the magazine. "Is it possible for one person to be this . . . this brilliant?"

Emma shrugged. "Maybe the brilliant person is the one who thought up the characters in the first place."

"But can anybody really be that observant? To see so much detail that everybody else misses? And to . . ." He paused to flip open to the marked page and search for a word. ". . . to deduce. Can someone actually deduce so much from only little bits of information?" He placed the magazine on the table.

"Dr. Doyle must think it's possible. He certainly makes Holmes and Watson sound believable, doesn't he?"

"Sure does." Ford rubbed his eyes and stretched. "I guess I better stack the wood before it gets dark." He headed out the back door, oblivious to Emma's expression of amused resignation. As soon as he disappeared, she smiled. Ford usually spent his afternoons trying to bury her in conversation, but since the newest *Strand* magazine arrived, he'd been uncommonly quiet.

The chores might not get done, but I do enjoy the silence. She began to hum as she finished setting the table. Shifting the magazine out of the way, she paused to thumb through the pages. Allowing Ford to read the latest adventures of her favorite detective had been the ultimate sacrifice, but after he went to bed, she planned to sit up and lose herself somewhere in the vicinity of 221B Baker Street.

Ford was right about Sherlock Holmes, though. Solid deductive reasoning through shrewd observation. Doyle did know how to approach a mystery.

No mysteries in Margin. She sighed. There was nothing to interest someone like Sherlock Holmes.

Except for Silas's cracker thief. (A hungry raccoon, she'd bet.)

Except for the strange Mr. Kirk who could get drunk on only one Saturday night whiskey and whose hangover always lasted until Monday.

Except for the sheriff's new fondness for vocabulary.

It puzzled Emma to discover such an unexpected facet to the man's personality. Johnny Callaghan had always been just a bit better spoken than some of the monosyllabic men in town. Of course, it didn't take an extensive vocabulary to say "Hello" and "Goodbye," which had been the sum total of their conversations.

Until today . . .

When she'd walked into the office, she hadn't expected the sheriff to defend his mistake quite so eloquently. Even more importantly, she hadn't expected his proximity to unnerve her quite as much as it had.

Well . . . actually, she might have guessed she'd get a bit flustered in his presence; she usually was. But for once, he seemed to be aware of her. He looked at her, really looked at her.

Twice.

In his office.

And at the bar.

He'd surprised her when he seemed reluctant to shoot Old Matilda, an action he'd taken countless times before. And Emma most certainly didn't expect him to turn around and correct Earl Gage, a man who absorbed words like a leaky sponge, dribbling out the wrong ones at the most interesting times. Since Earl was the head of the town's education committee, even Emma hadn't seen fit to correct his improper usage.

I wonder if Johnny is picking up his new vocabulary from Mr. Kirk. The man seems awfully well edu—

"Emma . . ." The back door slammed and Ford appeared in the kitchen, interrupting her thoughts. "Wood's stacked. Is supper ready?"

"Yes. Make sure you—"

"Wash my hands," he supplied. "Did already, outside."

She waited until he was well into his meal before broaching the subject which had commanded her thoughts earlier. "Uh . . . Ford, have you noticed anything . . . odd about Mr. Kirk?"

"Harvey? No, not really. He's pretty nice—for a drunk. He's smart, too."

Emma couldn't help but smirk. "Not smart enough to stay away from the bottle. Does the sheriff arrest him every Saturday night?"

Ford picked up a biscuit and slathered it with butter. "Sometimes the sheriff goes into the Crystal Plume to get him, and sometimes Harvey just shows up all by himself at the jail."

"Oh, speaking of the sheriff . . ." She reached into her dress pocket and pulled out the nickel. "He wanted me to give you this. You really *do* understand about the silver dollar, don't you?"

Her brother's ears reddened. "Yeah . . ." He released a ragged breath. "I thought it was odd when he gave me that much. I should have known it was a mistake."

Emma smiled inwardly, feeling a surge of near-parental pride for this rare display of maturity. "Well, Sheriff Callaghan said to tell you this was a bonus, not an advance." She allowed the smile to reach her face. "Does that make it a little better?"

Ford nodded. "I guess." He picked at the crumbs on the table, then after a brief moment, glanced up at her. "Emma, something . . . something strange happened today."

She felt small prickles rise on the back of her neck.

"What?"

"The sheriff started acting odd today."

The prickles increased, becoming goose bumps.

Ford continued, "When Old Matilda came a-courting again, Earl sent—"

She raised an eyebrow at her brother. "You mean Mr. Gage?" They might not be living in Tennessee anymore, but her brother would be raised with the manners befitting a Southern gentleman.

Ford reddened again. "When *Mister* Gage sent me to fetch help, Sheriff Callaghan looked like he didn't know what I was talking about. And then . . ." He lost his flush of embarrassment and leaned closer to his sister with conspiracy lighting his face. "Harv—Mr. Kirk told me to run along, and the sheriff would be there in a minute."

"So?"

"It wasn't right." He stared blankly across

the table. "I can't put my finger on it, but I know something wasn't right."

"What did the sheriff do after that?"

"Ran down to the Crystal Plume and shot a load of rock salt in her rump."

Emma dabbed at her lips with a napkin. "I know. I saw the commotion and peeped in." She glanced at Ford's empty plate and gestured for him to take his dishes to the sink.

As he got up, his chair scraped across the floor, leaving a faint mark on the wood. Emma glared at the scratch, then at her brother. "Do I need to get a bag of rock salt, young man?"

"No, Emma." He had the audacity to grin. "We don't have a shotgun."

"Don't need a shotgun. I could just—" She swatted at him as he carried his plate to the sink, but he danced out of her reach. "—use the bag all by itself."

Heading to the hallway, he paused and reached for the magazine sitting on the edge of the table.

Emma shook her head. "Homework first."

Ford grimaced, then placed the magazine reverently on the sideboard. Halfway down the hall, she heard him say, "I hate having my sister as my teacher."

"Terrible, isn't it?" she responded loudly. As soon as she heard his door close, she rushed the dishes to the sink, carefully dried her hands, then settled at the kitchen table with the magazine.

"All right, Mr. Holmes." She adjusted the wick of the kerosene lamp to combat the falling darkness. "Amaze me with your deductions."

Aching feet slowed Barrett's trip up the stairs. He paused at the landing to adjust his boot, then unbuckled his holster with listless fingers. Entering the room, he automatically slapped at the wall beside the door, looking for a light switch which didn't exist in this century.

"Damn!"

A voice echoed in answer through the shadows. "What's the old saying? It's better to light a candle than curse the dark?"

Barrett's heart took an extra beat.

Harvey.

Barrett cleared his throat. "How can I light a candle when I can't even see to find one?" He barely caught his balance after knocking into a chair.

"Allow me." The butane lighter flared for a moment, then the lamp flooded the room with a soft yellow light. Johnny's notes covered the desk where Harvey sat.

"Interesting reading material?" Barrett limped to the bed and groaned as he fell backward onto the feather mattress. "I don't think I've ever felt this tired before in my entire life."

Harvey nodded. "I know what you mean. I'm from L.A. and I don't know which was worse when I got here, the effects of the high altitude or breathing air you can't see." He grinned. "And yes, these notes are quite interesting . . . if you discount Johnny's rather unique way of spelling things."

Barrett fumbled with the buttons of his shirt. "All I want is a hot shower and maybe something quick to eat. Then I've got to get some sleep."

"Uh-oh."

Barrett rolled over and squinted at Harvey. "What do you mean, 'uh-oh'?"

"No showers. Especially not hot ones. You'll have to wait until Saturday for your bath."

"Saturday?" Barrett tried to struggle to a sitting position but gave up halfway. "No shower. No fast food. It's like living in the dark ages."

"Ah yes . . ." Harvey adopted a satisfied grin. "But the food here, however slow, is good. Our inimitable landlady Miss Penny will no doubt have her typical spread ready in about a half hour." The man pushed up from the chair and moved toward the door. "It might not be as tasty as a Big Mick, but you'll find it a treat."

Barrett stared at Harvey. "Don't you mean a Big Mac?"

"They haven't called it that since Disney bought out McDon—" Harvey stopped suddenly, then reddened. "Forget you heard that, okay? I . . . I'll see you at supper."

Barrett managed to remove his boots before tugging at the blanket to cover him where he lay. Sleep belied its gentle nature, seizing him by the throat and forcing him to surrender to his overwhelming exhaustion.

The next morning, he awoke not sure where he was. Staring at the cracked ceiling above him, he had the location down to two possibilities: a cheap hotel room in Barcelona, or a bed and breakfast somewhere in the Smoky Mountains near Gatlinburg. Neither room had boasted what one might describe as an ergonomically-correct bed.

Barrett stretched, then threw back the blanket, revealing his costume.

It's not a costume.

The present blended with the future and the past for one explosive moment of confusion, then awareness.

Margin.

Barrett stumbled to his feet and found a fresh basin of water, a clean towel, and a tiny sliver of brown soap on the washstand. Stripping to his long johns, he did the best job he could washing off the topmost layer of grime, then found a fresh shirt hanging from a peg in the wardrobe. After he dressed, he trailed the aroma of coffee, following it down the front stairs and into a noisy dining room.

"Good morning, Sheriff." A large, frowsy woman greeted him with a strained smile. "Up a bit later'n usual, aren't you?"

He shrugged, trying to make his sluggish brain remember her name. He stared out the large picture window and read the letters painted on the glass. ESUOH GNIDRAOB S'YNNEP SSIM. *Miss Penny's Boarding House*.

"Morning, Miss Penny." He rubbed the back of his neck. "I went to bed with a headache last night, and I guess I needed a bit of extra sleep."

She led him to an empty table. "Well I figgered it was something like that, seein' how we had fried chicken last night and you seldom miss your favorite meal. I bet you're hungry now! You want your usual?"

Barrett nodded, for the lack of anything else to do.

Ten minutes later, he stared down into a large plate of calories, cholesterol, and fat. Another ten minutes later, he admired the pattern printed on the bottom of the empty plate. In his world, breakfast either came through the car window in a bag or out of the freezer in a microwave-proof tray. Neither version tasted as decadently real as the meal he had just consumed.

A man could get used to this . . .

He pushed back in his chair and drank his second cup of steaming black coffee. Caffeine and all.

"My goodness, Johnny." Miss Penny glided to his table, perching her large hand on the edge of the checkered cloth. The coffee sloshed as the tabletop shifted downward. "I don't think I've ever seen you eat so fast!"

Barrett rescued his cup and gave her a self-conscious smile. "I guess I was extra hungry. It was delicious."

"Well I do so like to see a man enjoy his food." An indelicate flush colored her face. "I-I know you're going to be busy today, what with it bein' payday and such, so I'll send lunch to the office around eleven. All right?"

"Uh, thanks." Barrett wiped his mouth on the red gingham napkin, stood, and headed toward the door. He was afraid to look back at what he feared were Miss Penny's lovelorn glances drilling into his back.

Out on the street, the townspeople were moving at a faster clip than the day before. Yesterday, Silas the grocer had a couple of chairs and several barrels sitting on the porch in front of his store. Today, the sidewalk was bare. The proud peacock sign was gone from the Crystal Plume, leaving a couple of empty chains to swing free in the mild breeze. A guard stood in plain view in the bank entrance, unlocking the door to let customers in and out.

What the hell's going on? Johnny didn't mention anything special about payday. Barrett dodged a couple of wagons to make it across the street to the newspaper office. The front page sat in the window on display, the headlines screaming in large type:

DEADLY COMBINATIONS?

Margin prepares for a difficult few days when payday falls on Saturday this month. Businesses are warned to protect themselves from the drunken horde of miners soon to descend on our fair town. Last time, it took a week to clean up. This time, general store owner Silas Brainard reports he has enough glass in stock to return the town to business by Monday.

All townspeople interested in being deputized for the duration of this situation should report to the sheriff's office by nine a.m. Saturday morning for their ammunition and assignments.

A man wearing an ink-stained apron knocked on the window from the inside, catching Barrett's attention. The printer pulled out his pocket watch and gestured to the time. "Almost nine," he mouthed.

Barrett nodded his thanks, pivoted, and headed back to his office. Ammunition and assignments? He was definitely in over his head, and he didn't believe quick thinking or a great imagination would do much to help. Only one person could help.

Harvey!

He spotted the time-traveler sitting on the stairs outside the office. Judging by the people crowding in the doorway, the building was packed.

"Harvey, I—"

"Shut up and get over here." Harvey grabbed him by the sleeve and hauled him over to the side alley. "I know Johnny didn't mention this, but—"

"But payday falls on Saturday this month," Barrett offered. "And the miners are going to get drunk and try to tear up the town."

The man's jaw dropped for a moment, then he nodded with growing appreciation. "You're getting the hang of this. Okay, here's the game plan. Tell the guys to take their usual assignments. And for heaven's sake, warn 'em not to shoot if they don't have to. Last time, half the glass was broken by a couple of trigger-happy townspeople shooting at shadows."

"Got it." Barrett turned to head back for the office but paused. "And thanks for the help, Harvey. I think I'll be needing a lot of advice." Barrett pushed his way into the office and the noise level dropped appreciably.

"Gentlemen, I'm glad to see you." It was a standard opening line from a thousand board meetings he'd conducted. He gave them a sincere but tight-lipped smile, something he'd perfected during the early days when he thought he could still save his company from bankruptcy. "We won't make many changes from the last time this happened. You know your assignments. And . . . I won't name names, but let me caution you about shooting. You don't shoot unless you absolutely have to, do you understand?"

The men were split into two factions, some arguing about the protection of hearth and home and others reluctantly agreeing to a no-shoot order. The grocer nodded as well, but he wore a pained look as if he was calculating how much money he had tied up in a large inventory of pane glass which might go unused.

A dark-haired man wearing a badge called the group to attention. "Now you heard what Johnny said. So line up and get deputized."

The men formed a ragged line, and Barrett used the opportunity to corral Harvey into a corner. "Who's this guy?" he whispered, nodding toward the man handing out tin stars.

"Your deputy, Jimmie Soames. You didn't meet him yesterday because it was his day off."

"Oh." Barrett watched the men file out of the office after receiving their instructions.

"He's a good man," Harvey whispered. "Not too bright, but conscientious."

After the last man left, Jimmie pivoted and shook his head. "I've got a feelin' in my bones about this one."

Barrett perched on the corner of the desk. "A good feeling or a bad one?"

The man shivered. "Bad one. Good feelings never make your bones ache. Not only is it Saturday and payday, but the *Farmer's Almanac* says it's a full moon tonight. And you know how squirrelly these miners can get under a full moon. Well . . ." He reached down and secured the leather thong at the bottom of his holster, tying it around his leg. "I'll go make a final round and make sure everybody's in place. You want second shift, Johnny?"

"Uh . . . sure. That'll be fine."

The young man all but swaggered as he strode out of the office. He paused in the doorway, silhouetted by the glare of the morning sun. "I just feel it in my bones . . ." He disappeared.

Barrett sighed. "Harvey, whatever you do, don't tell me Jimmie's psychic."

"Not psychic." Harvey pulled out his watch and reached into its depths to remove a cigar. He bit a piece off the end and expertly spat the tobacco tip into a brass spittoon by the door. "But he's right. There's . . ." Harvey stared toward the sun-brightened window, then shivered. "There's a feeling in the air. It's been too quiet for the last few Saturday nights."

Barrett tried to shake off the disconcerting chill which danced along the collar of his shirt. An abrupt thought lit the back of his mind. "Wait . . . if *tonight's* Saturday, what were you doing in the jail yesterday? I didn't think Friday was your day to commune with the future."

"No mystery." The flame from Harvey's lighter licked the end of the cigar. "It was my mother's birthday, and I wanted to jump forward and give her a present." When Barrett's gaze settled a bit too long on the man, Harvey returned the glare from behind a cloud of smoke. "Don't look at me so funny. I'm human, just like you. I *do* have a mom, you know."

"How comforting," Barrett grumbled. "So what do we do about the miners? Bar them from town?"

"Good God, no!" Harvey kept the cigar firmly clenched in his teeth. "They're a major source of revenue for the town. Margin couldn't exist without them."

Barrett fanned away the plume of smoke which tried to drift toward him. "Seems like the town can't live with them, either. So when do we expect this shooting match to begin?"

Harvey shrugged, creating another cloud which hung above his head like a gray halo. "How long does it take a thirsty man to finish his first whiskey?"

Emma shifted, sending the rocker into motion. The fire crackled, casting flickery shadows that danced on her cabin floor.

So far, so good.

She'd lived through one Saturday payday before, but as Deputy Soames had mentioned to her earlier in the day, there was something different in the air tonight. Back in Chattanooga, she'd once seen a tornado choose a random path through town, leaving death and devastation in its wake.

The miners weren't as deadly, but they could be almost as destructive, especially after dark.

They had a penchant for breaking windows, which necessitated heavy drapes to hide the telltale light from within. The curtains also muted the noise of their drunken laughter, much to Emma's relief.

How can Ford sleep through all that noise?

The last time the miners came to town under the flag of a triple threat, she and Ford had sat up and played games to pass the time. Both had been too nervous to sleep.

This time, her brother merely wished her a hurried good-night and disappeared into his room.

It grew suddenly quiet outside, lulling Emma into a momentary sense of well-being. *It's ov—*

A gunshot split the silence, then several voices broke into a rather coarse song about a young lady's bloomers. Emma blushed, wondering if she'd hear her brother whistling the song the next day. He couldn't possibly sleep through the racket outside.

The awful truth struck her suddenly like a cold rag in the face. Going into Ford's room merely confirmed the fact. He wasn't asleep.

He was gone.

Ford was outside.

Somewhere.

Emma warmed her shaking hands by the fire. She knew she had to find him, but only one type of unescorted woman dared walk the streets of Margin on a night like this.

And that type of female didn't stay by herself for long.

Nor was she a lady.

It wouldn't be prudent, Emma decided, to wander the streets looking for her brother, but she would need to venture out in order to alert the sheriff. Emma glanced at the clock on the mantel. Nine-fifteen. Sheriff Callaghan was probably sitting on the balcony overlooking the main floor of the Crystal Plume, shotgun in hand.

Emma mentally navigated the safest route to the saloon, avoiding those places where danger might lurk in the form of a drunken miner. It would be difficult, but she prayed she could do it.

She'd need some help.

With a sigh of uneasy resignation, Emma went into her bedroom and retrieved the last present her father ever gave her: a Derringer. She remembered his instructions:

"A little gun like this won't frighten a man, so don't try to wave it in his face and threaten him. And if you shoot him from a distance, it won't stop him . . . probably only make him mad. Just leave it in your bag and when he gets close enough, just reach through the material, point the gun, and pull the trigger. It won't kill him, but it just may make him think twice about bothering you."

Emma loaded the gun, then gingerly placed it into her least favorite drawstring purse made of a flowered chintz. If she was forced to pull the trigger, there was no use shooting a hole through her fondest purse. She pulled on her grey cloak, hoping the neutral-colored material would help her to blend with the shadows and not draw attention to herself. After turning the lamp wick down low, she ventured outside.

Each shriek of laughter, each scream,

made her jump, but the eerie periods of silence worried her the most. The mind's eye painted danger around each corner, lecherous men waiting to pounce on the unsuspecting. With her nerves attuned to respond to even the smallest sound, she slowly made her way to the saloon.

She decided the back staircase would be the most judicious way to get into the building. But she hesitated, not relishing a trip through the upstairs hall, where one could hear the moans and grunts of satisfied customers in the expert hands of "The Ladies."

Emma always thought the title was a bit pretentious, a convenient pretense to save more delicate churchgoing ears from the use of the word, "prostitute." But, for the life of her, Emma couldn't condemn "The Ladies" for making whatever life they could in a world which treated single women with so little concern.

As she tiptoed down the hallway, the boisterous revelers in the saloon thankfully drowned out the sounds of unbridled passion coming from "The Ladies'" rooms. Peering from around the door frame, she spotted Johnny sitting in a straight-backed chair, shotgun balanced across his lap.

He seemed to be scanning the crowd with rapt attention, more fascinated than wary.

"Sheriff." The noise of the crowd swallowed the word. She spoke louder, hoping to get his attention without anyone else's notice. "Sheriff!"

He turned and stared at her for a moment. "Emma . . . what are you doing here?"

She motioned for him to come into the corridor; she certainly didn't want anyone else to see her, especially since she had just tiptoed through a brothel to get there.

"It's Ford."

The sheriff stood and moved toward the doorway. "What about him?"

"He's missing!"

Johnny took a moment to digest her revelation. "You mean . . . you mean he's out here somewhere?"

Why was the man acting so thickheaded? "Yes. Apparently Ford snuck out after supper. I thought he'd gone to bed."

"Well I'm sure he's all right—"

She felt her hands tighten into fists. "Sheriff Callaghan! He's only eleven! A child lost in the middle of a nightmare straight out of Dante's *Inferno!*"

The sheriff had the audacity to shoot her a pained smile. "I suppose it does have a sort of 'Abandon hope all ye who enter here' look to it."

Her heart stopped. At least, that was what it felt like to her. This man, this uneducated lawman of a forgotten town deep in the

Rockies, was quoting Dante to her! "I . . .
uh . . . well—"

A whoop and a bellow interrupted her.

"Barlow, you ain't got the sense the Good
Lord gives a rock squirrel!" shouted an
anonymous voice from the saloon floor.
"You're dumber than a box of rocks!"

Emma peered around the sheriff. She saw
one grubby miner facing another, both with
fists raised. It reminded Emma of pictures
she'd seen of the prizefighter John L. Sulli-
van.

"Me dumb?" his opponent yelled. "You're
stoopider than . . . than . . . that stuffed
moose up there! And twice as ugly!"

"Ugly? I'll show you ugly!"

As the two men began to throw ineffective
punches, Emma spotted her brother, cower-
ing behind the bar. "There's Ford!" she
whispered frantically.

The sheriff scanned the room. "Where?"

"There." She pointed, watching her
brother try to crawl along the floor toward
the end of the bar.

Ford looked up, spotting her on the balcony. He offered her a quick, guilty grimace-
smile, then continued his trek across the
floor. Emma flinched as one miner threw
the other against the bar, almost showering
her brother with broken glass.

"He'll get killed!" She started toward the

stairs, stopped only by an iron grip on her arm.

Johnny's knuckles whitened. "You can't go down there!"

"I can't just stand here and watch this. *You* do something!"

"Uh . . ." He hesitated for a moment, drew a deep breath, then nodded. "Okay, I'll do . . . something." He shoved the shotgun at her. "Know how to use one of these?"

She gulped, then nodded, not quite ready to take the weapon.

"Good." Then, he added under his breath, "That makes one of us." He looked momentarily embarrassed, then raised his voice. "If things get much worse, point this thing at the ceiling and fire! Understand?"

Emma hesitated for only a moment before reaching out for the shotgun. "At the ceiling . . ." she repeated.

She watched the sheriff inch down the stairs toward the bar. The miners continued slamming into tables and chairs, and as they separated drinkers from their drinks, more men joined the fight. Emma split her attention between her brother, who was making slow but steady progress toward her, and Johnny, who displayed little of the spirit and courage she'd come to associate with the tough sheriff of Margin.

He recoiled at every shout or crash, whether the pieces of broken chairs landed nearby or not. Finally, the sheriff made it all the way down the stairs, and Ford rushed the last few feet to his rescuer. Emma watched helplessly as a pair of strapping miners lurched toward her brother, too absorbed in their fisticuffs to notice anybody else. Johnny pulled Ford out of the way, deflecting the blows himself.

Emma suddenly remembered the shotgun in her hands. She pointed it at the ceiling.

And fired.

One chunk of plaster hit her in the shoulder, then silence, like a gentle cloud of white powder, drifted through the room.

Finally, a lone voice spoke.

"Well . . . looky here, boys. We have a visitor."

Emma's finger tightened on the trigger.

"Ain't she a purty one?" added a second voice.

"I think I'm goin' to get me a little kiss from her."

The second man threw an elbow in the first one's ribs. "You ain't. I saw her first!"

"The hell you did!"

The fight started over again, lasting only for a few seconds until Emma remembered to fire a second round into the ceiling.

The first miner stared at her. "Two barrels." His expression changed to a lecherous grin. "Two shots." He started for the stairs.

Johnny intercepted the man by stepping

in front of him. "Just leave the lady alone and—"

The miner stiff-armed the sheriff. "Mind yer own biz'ness."

From her higher vantage point, Emma continued to track the miner in her sights, then realized her empty gun was no threat. And according to her late father, neither was the Derringer in the purse dangling from her right hand.

"I said *No!*" Johnny took a swing at the man, connecting with a bristled jaw.

The man's head snapped to the side, then he turned back, giving the sheriff a look of mild amusement. Then the man balled one meaty fist and knocked the sheriff into the bar. Johnny slid to the floor in a lifeless heap.

Emma watched the miner start for the stairs.

His licentious grin sported a gold tooth. "Might as well drop the shotgun, little lady. We don't need it where we're gonna go." He lumbered up the stairs, pointing beyond her to the infamous corridor behind her.

Emma dropped the useless gun and fumbled with her bag, backing toward the corridor. She hit a hard flesh wall and heard a silky voice in her ear.

"Where you headed, pretty lady?"

Another one? She rammed an elbow backward into the interloper's stomach, hoping to sidestep him and retreat through the brothel. Although he was bent over double, the man latched onto her arm and pulled her closer. She smelled the whiskey on his soured breath.

Broken teeth filled Whiskey-Breath's grin. "Not so fast, honey!"

The miner from downstairs appeared on the landing. "Wait a minute. I saw her first!"

Whiskey-Breath pulled her closer. "But I've got her," he taunted.

The two men began to argue, jostling Emma as they punctuated their remarks with flying fists. She recoiled from the punches as she reached for her bag, unable to find the trigger. In the midst of the threats and grunts, she heard Ford's anguished cry.

"Leave my sister alone!"

All she needed was Ford to join in this donnybrook. She scrambled to find the Derringer, finally feeling the gun's trigger through the fabric. The shot went wild, but at least the men stopped their fight.

Whiskey-Breath wrenched the bag from her grasp and pulled out the Derringer. Cradled in his large hand, the small pistol looked more like a child's toy than a real weapon. "You might hurt somebody iffin' you don't watch out." He tossed the gun toward the stairs, then drew out a revolver with an impossibly long barrel. "Now one look at *this* and a wise man'll stop in his tracks."

Emma heard thundering footfalls as if someone were taking the stairs two steps at a time. She struggled with her smelly captor. "No, Ford!" she managed to scream before a flannel-clad arm clamped over her throat.

Another face loomed into view, the miner from downstairs. "I said I saw her first," he slurred, pulling her arm. A red haze choked off her sight and a rush of blood filled her ears. Suddenly, a loud explosion overwhelmed the roar. The arm loosened, allowing her to draw a shuddering breath.

Whiskey-Breath's voice grew solemn. "You jackass . . . you shot him!"

Ford!

She twisted out of the man's grasp and knocked him out of the way as she ran toward the stairs, expecting to see her brother lying on the landing. But instead of her brother, she saw Johnny leaning against the wall at the landing. Pushing past the sheriff, she almost stumbled as she rushed down to the saloon. "Ford, where are you?"

Ford stood up from his hiding place behind the bar. "Here. I-I'm all right."

Emma grabbed him in a tight embrace, sending up a prayer of thanks for his deliverance from danger. "I thought . . . I mean, when I realized—" She stopped suddenly and held him back at arm's length, reassuring herself he was indeed unharmed. "Ford . . . if you're not hurt, then who . . . ?" Turning around, she glanced up at Johnny, who hadn't moved from his position near the top of the stairs.

The sheriff withdrew his hand from his vest and stared at the blood coating his fingers. His face paled, then he stepped away from the wall, revealing a red stain marring the striped wallpaper. He gave her a weak grin, then slowly sagged until he sprawled over the balustrade.

Four

Barrett felt fire cutting through him, robbing him of breath as well as the ability to think straight. At first, he had only been numb, not even sure he was hurt at all. But once helping hands clumsily lifted him from the floor, the floodgates of pain opened.

He tried to focus on a pale face swimming in a gray haze above him. It was Emma Nolan. Her mouth moved, but the words made no sense. However, her strained smile gave him a vague feeling of reassurance, a sense of well-being which allowed him to close his eyes, knowing he just might live to open them again some day.

When he did reopen his eyes, he didn't recognize the man hovering over him.

"Who . . . are you?" Why was it so difficult to talk?

Another voice spoke. "He's delirious."

Barrett realized someone else was in the room.

"He don't even recognize you, Lemuel. You

got to do something quick!" It was Jimmie
Soames, the deputy.

Barrett knew he had to push past the pain
and jump-start his brain. He was in Margin.
It was 1892. And the man named Lemuel
was . . . was the barber. "S-sorry, Lemuel.
Didn't recognize you for a moment."

"That's all right, Sheriff." The barber's
head bobbed up and down and he pursed
his thin lips. "I've done this a thousand
times before, so don't worry."

"D-done what?" Barrett blinked, trying to
focus on Lemuel's face.

The man picked up a knife with a shaky
hand. "Give him the strap to bite down on,
Jimmie. We'll have that bullet out in no
time."

Barrett intercepted the leather thong before it could be shoved in his mouth. "No
anesthesia?"

The barber stared blankly at him. "No
what?"

"Anesthesia. Something to knock me out
so I don't feel the pain."

A nervous smile erupted across Lemuel's
face. "Don't worry. After the first few minutes, most of my patients usually pass out,
anyway." The knife jiggled as it loomed
closer.

You mean, your victims! Barrett drew a deep,
painful breath, feeling a resurgence of sticky

warmth flow out of him. "No. I want a doctor. A real doctor."

Lemuel stared at him. "What the hell you talkin' about, Sheriff? I'm the only 'doctor' around these parts." The blade trembled as it caught the light.

"No!" Barrett struggled to a sitting position, but he gave up as the room began to darken and spin. "You're not touching me. I want a real doctor. A surgeon with credentials. Not some medieval barber with a dull stone knife and leeches."

The man flushed and the knife cha-chaed through the air. "He's got brain fever, Jimmie. It's probably lead poisoning from the bullet in his gut. Iffin' I don't get it out soon, he's a goner."

"You lay one finger on me and my attorney'll have you for lunch. I'll sic the A.M.A. on you for practicing without a license. Hell, I'll call 'Sixty Minutes'!" A fresh raw pain split his attention and the room took a lurch to the right. He reached up and got a fistful of the deputy's shirt. "Get him out of here, Jimmie. With his Neanderthal scalpels and . . ." It grew harder to draw a breath. "Now," he rasped.

Jimmie pulled the man away. "Lemuel, why don't you step outside for a moment?"

"But he'll die—"

"Lemuel, just give me a minute."

The two men shared a knowing glance, then the barber nodded and disappeared.

"Okay Johnny, you can calm down." Jimmie gave him a weak smile. "He's gone for now, but you *know* you don't have any other choice. You gotta let Lemuel try to get th' bullet out of you."

"The operative word is *try*. I don't want someone to *try*, I want someone to *succeed*."

"But there's not another doctor around here for miles except . . . er . . ." The deputy's expression clouded, a secret blotting out the sense of concern in his gaze.

"Except who? Anybody's better than that quack."

A blush turned Jimmie's ears a bright red. "Maybe not. After all, it's only a rumor, and who knows if it's really true. Anyways, it ain't proper . . ." His voice trailed off as his face reddened even more.

"Rumor? What? Who?"

Jimmie ducked his head. "The schoolmistress," he muttered.

Barrett clawed through the red haze blunting his ability to think. "Schoolteacher . . . Emma? She's a doctor?"

The deputy ran a hand across the back his neck. "I know, I know. It was a stupid idea." He lowered himself into a chair and leaned forward with a gleam of confusion and conspiracy in his eyes. "But I heard it from my wife, who said the minister's wife said—"

Barrett gripped the deputy's arm. "I don't care who said what. All I want to know is: Is she or isn't she a doctor?"

A voice came from across the room.

"I am."

Emma swam into focus, her stern but competent face filling him with a guarded sense of relief. "I'll admit I don't have any formal study, but my father did, and he taught me everything he knew." She clutched a well-worn black bag and drew to her full height. "I've operated before."

"Oh yeah? On who?" Jimmie challenged.

Emma leveled the deputy with one chilling gray glance. "My brother, for one." She turned toward Barrett. "Ford was in a carriage wreck when he was seven and required surgery for his injuries. My father had broken his hand in the same accident and couldn't perform. So I operated under his supervision."

Jimmie took a brave step forward. "But your daddy ain't here to tell you what to do anymore."

"Correct. But my father recognized my skills, and after Ford's recovery I was allowed to work without being monitored. In the course of my practice, I've removed bullets, sewn up knife wounds, set broken bones, treated all manners of disease, and saved several lives."

Barrett followed her glance to Lemuel's

collection of blunt razors and used bandages, and they both shuddered. When she turned to face him, Barrett looked into her blue eyes and read honesty, determination, and best of all, competence in her steeled stare. He reached for her hand. "You really know what to do?"

Warm fingers wrapped around his cold ones. "Yes, I do, Sheriff."

Barrett struggled to draw a breath, finding the process becoming more difficult. "Jimmie, come here." His own voice began to sound thready and weak.

The deputy sprang to the bedside. "Yes, Sheriff?"

"You're my witness. Miss Nolan will be my surgeon. You keep that palsied beautician Lemuel away from me, you hear? And if . . . if something happens and I don't pull through—" He gestured for Jimmie to be quiet before the agitated man could raise a protest. "—you make sure no one blames Miss Nolan for my death. Understand?"

"But Johnny—"

"That's an order, Deputy Soames."

The man nodded reluctantly. "Yes, sir."

Barrett tried to give Emma's hand a squeeze, but his strength failed. "Miss Nolan, please . . . tell me you know what the word 'anesthesia' means."

Emma gave him a persuasive grin. "I even know how to spell it." She turned his hand over and began to take his pulse, a professional gesture which did even more to reassure him. "I have ether with me and I'm familiar with its proper administration."

The room began to spin and the black dots spotting his vision started to swell and fill in his sight. "Hold off, Doc. You might not need any . . ."

Emma scrubbed her hands hard, perhaps even harder than she had before the operation. Using a small brush, she removed all traces of Johnny's blood from her fingers and palms, then dried her hands on a clean towel. She gave herself time to stretch and flex tense muscles before returning to her duties at Johnny's bedside.

She pulled back the sheet which draped his bare torso, then gently peeled back the bandage and checked for signs of infection. Streaks of red marred the skin around the edges of the puckered wound. She sighed and reached for her supplies. Despite her best precautions during the surgery, there was still a chance infection could spell doom for the otherwise healthy sheriff. Johnny could thank Lemuel the barber and his soiled rags for creating a problem with which she had to deal now.

She tried to concentrate on cleaning out the wound rather than admiring his broad, bared chest. During the operation she'd had no problem paying attention to the important task at hand. But now that she had the bullet resting on a pad of cotton wool, she was once again reminded of his undeniable masculinity by the extra thump to her heartbeat when she caught sight of him.

Emma couldn't help but stare at him, telling herself her interest in his physique was purely a matter of appreciating the male anatomy in general.

She allowed herself a sigh.

Or Johnny's anatomy in particular.

She'd seen bigger, stronger men before, but there was something in the way he was built, a coiled strength held in reserve, latent but powerful. He was a man who held the peace together with a great deal of wisdom, a bit of humor, and an occasional display of restrained power. Yet for all the slings and arrows of life's journey, his skin was strangely unmarked. No scars. No evidence of previous wounds. Surely, as a lawman, he'd faced some dangers in his career. But there were no signs.

An expression of discomfort crossed his sleeping face. He shifted, then grimaced, muttering incoherently. Emma placed a hand on his brow, startled by the building heat in his skin.

Confound that barber. He may have killed you, yet. She sprang from her chair and headed toward the door. "Miss Penny!" she shouted down the hall. "Come here quickly, I need you!"

Emma could feel the room shake as the large woman thundered up the stairs.

"What's wrong?" the woman panted. "Is he all right? What do you need?"

"The sheriff's running a fever and it seems to be getting worse. I need cold water and towels. We've got to cool him down."

The woman shouldered her aside and placed one meaty hand in the center of his bared chest. "I think you should—"

"Miss Penny . . ." Emma stopped the woman with one calculated, glacial stare. "I'm in charge here and I know what I'm doing. Just get me what I need and you'll be doing your part in saving this man's life."

Miss Penny removed her hand with a self-conscious blush. "I suppose you're right. I'll go . . ." Her voice trailed off as she seemed mesmerized once more by the sight of the half-naked man in the bed.

"Hurry, Miss Penny." Emma shoved the woman toward the door.

At the sound of feet pounding down the stairs, Emma stared at her patient. She pulled off the sheet which covered his lower body, revealing a strategically placed towel tucked across his narrow hips. The deputy had insisted on undressing the sheriff, deeming it a task unfit for a lady. *I hope you forgive me for this, Johnny . . .*

Three hours later, the sheriff's temperature was still rising and he began to thrash and moan. Miss Penny had even gotten over her terminal blush and helped to exchange cool towels for the ones warmed by his inextinguishable fever.

After one particularly violent episode, Emma dropped to her knees on the floor by his bed. "I don't know what to do, Penny. If I don't bring this fever down, he won't survive. How can I cool him off?"

Even the unflappable Miss Penny sounded tired. "You can't, child. You've done your best. It's up to the Good Lord, now."

Emma placed her cheek against the wet mattress. "You mean leave it up to the undertaker." She shivered at the thought of losing Johnny.

"Now Emma, Mr. Bellwood's only performing his duty," the woman offered.

"So what am I supposed to do? Just stand back and let that vulture bring his made-to-measure coffin up here and hover around waiting for the sheriff to die?" Her shiver turned into violent tremors as she pictured Johnny stretched out in a pine box.

Then the image changed.

Not dead, but immersed in cold water.

Emma clutched the edge of the bed.

"Penny, get Bellwood up here. Tell him to haul up that cursed coffin, right now!"

The large woman bent down and patted Emma's shoulder. "Poor dear . . . this has been too much for you, hasn't it? I always said women weren't cut out for—"

"Be quiet and listen to me, Penny." Emma felt the hope build, eradicating the gloom which had held her soul hostage only moments before. "We put Johnny in the casket and fill it up with cold water. Snow, if we can get it. There must be some up in the high country. It'll work . . . I know it'll work."

After Mr. Bellwood arrived, his solemn features didn't even twitch as Emma proposed her idea. He merely nodded and crossed to the window to signal his apprentice, who had the dubious honor of carrying up the heavy wooden box made to Johnny's exact dimensions. Penny coordinated a bucket brigade, and Emma manned the last bucket, pouring the water over Johnny's flushed body lying in the sheet-lined casket, his head elevated by a sodden pillow.

After the last pail, she checked the poultice and oilskin bandage she'd concocted to protect his wound from the water. To her relief, it remained watertight.

Using a washrag, she bathed his face, watching him carefully. He muttered and even occasionally splashed her as he relived various memories, some good, some evidently bad.

"Where's the remote? I can't watch TV without the remote."

She figured T.V. must be someone's initials, but wasn't sure what a "remote" was. She used her most soothing voice to reassure him. "Everything's all right, Johnny. I'm sure T.V. will be fine."

"Lousy season. No good shows . . ." His voice trailed off as his face relaxed. But in a few minutes, he became agitated again. His strong hand latched onto her arm.

"I don't want to fly to Pittsburgh. I hate flying . . ."

Flying? He must be in worse shape than I thought. It took her some time to pry his strong fingers from her arm. She noticed a pale band on his right ring finger, as if he had worn a ring for a long time and had only recently removed it. *No time for curiosities.* Emma tested the water's temperature, wondering if it was still cool enough to do him any good. Then she dried off her hand and cupped his cheek, measuring his temperature.

"How's he doing?" Released from his bucket brigade duty, Jimmie Soames stood in the doorway with his hat in his hand.

Emma jerked her hand back, feeling as if she'd been caught doing something she shouldn't have. "Better, I think. The fever may have broken."

"You look exhausted. How long have you been up?"

She sat on the floor, uncaring if she appeared ungainly. "I don't know. I can't even tell you what day it is."

He played with the brim of his hat. "It's Tuesday."

Emma couldn't even manage the energy to gawk at him. "What happened to Sunday? I don't seem to remember it at all."

He looked up at her for the first time. "They say it was the only time you've missed church since you moved here."

"I hope the townspeople prayed for him." She stared down at her sleeping patient.

Jimmie nodded. "They did. Preacher said some mighty nice things about Sheriff Callaghan."

"Well, all those good thoughts did some good. His fever broke."

The deputy glanced at the near-naked man lying in the coffin. "You . . . you want help getting him out of there?"

Emma nodded. "Please."

Between the two of them, they managed to grasp the sheet and lift Johnny out without disturbing his wound. As Jimmie dried the sheriff off, Emma examined her handiwork, removing the poultice and bandage and checking for infection. The red streaks had faded, and she saw the initial evidence of healing. A tremor coursed through the patient, and while she wrapped him in a quilt, she dealt with her own quaking pangs of guilt.

She charged herself with his survival not merely as a doctor, but as the person ultimately responsible for his predicament. Johnny Callaghan was fighting for his life because of her brother. And she was responsible for Ford's actions. It was as simple as that.

You'll live, Johnny Callaghan. Because I won't let you die.

Barrett pried open his eyes, wincing as the light from the window stabbed the back of his brain.

I'm hung over . . .

"Johnny . . . you awake?"

It was a soft voice. A familiar voice.

A female voice.

What did I do last night? It was like a bad college memory come back to haunt him—the morning after the first smoker at the Theta house.

Barrett tried to roll over and see if there was another face staring at him from across the pillow. But pain stopped him. It started in his side and radiated out like lightning bolts, making black dots swell up and blot his vision.

"Don't try to move, Sheriff."

Sheriff? What is she—oh Good Lord . . . I'm still Johnny! "What happened?" His mouth didn't seem willing to respond to his brain. It came out "Whah h'pen?"

Emma appeared above him in a lavender-colored cloud. "You don't remember? You were shot."

"In the s'loon?"

She gave him a tired smile which betrayed her evident relief. "No, in your lower chest."

Barrett returned her grin, his mouth finally deciding to cooperate. "S-semantics . . . to a sick man. Ought to be 'shamed."

Her smile blossomed into something wide and sunny, helping to dispel the shudders of pain which continued to radiate through his body.

She released a deep, satisfied-sounding sigh. "Thank you, Johnny."

Somewhere in the back of his mind, he realized it was the first time she'd used his—Johnny's—first name. "W-why thank me?"

A note of concern dimmed her grin, turning it into a more solemn expression. "Because I'm glad all the foolishness didn't leak out through that hole in your side. If you can make me laugh, then I know you'll be fine."

The recent past began to trickle back

through his consciousness. His fingers found the edge of the large bandage swathing his ribs. "You didn't let that butcher operate on me, did you?" He had an unsettling vision of a dirty scalpel wielded by a trembling hand.

She smoothed the hair off his forehead, her touch electrifying his skin. "Don't worry, Johnny. *I* operated on you."

He felt relief course through him, taking the edge off the throbbing pain. The soft mattress seemed to rise up and swallow him, making the room spin.

"Johnny . . . Johnny? I have to ask you a question." Her voice began to fade away. "Why me? No, don't go to sleep yet. Tell me why you allowed me to oper . . ."

He surrendered to the noiseless void and slept.

"C'mon, Johnny. Open your mouth . . . that's a good boy."

Mom?

"You've got to get some of this soup inside you. We've spilled enough on the outside."

The warm broth slipped effortlessly down his throat. *Mom always takes such good care of . . .* He opened his eyes. *Not Mom.*

Emma.

She offered him a pleasant smile. "I swear you're the only man I've ever met who can eat in his sleep." She held the spoon to his lips, and he obediently accepted the liquid. For some reason, he noticed she wore yellow.

"You changed clothes." He nodded toward her gingham skirt.

"It was about time. I don't think you've been much aware of the passage of time. You've been out for a couple of days."

Barrett struggled to lift the edge of the thin blanket which covered him up to the waist. "And speaking of clothes . . . where are mine?"

"Washed, mended, ironed, folded and waiting for you to get better."

He could feel the color rising in his cheeks. "You could at least let me have my Jockeys."

She stared at him. "Your what?"

"My . . ." The proper word eluded him for a moment. "My long johns."

She shook her head. "I'm afraid the waistband will aggravate your wound. It's starting to heal nicely, and I don't want to do anything which might start another round of infections."

"What about catching my death of cold?" He pulled the blanket up to his chin, inadvertently exposing his toes in the process.

Emma made a face, carefully placed the bowl on the bedside, and moved to the end of the bed. With one violent jerk, the blanket slid down to his waist again. She tucked the material around the bottom of the mattress. Before he could protest, she reached below his line of sight and reappeared with a heavier quilt in her hands. As she spread the fabric over him, she had the audacity to grin. "I make it a practice not to let my recovering gunshot patients die of exposure."

"How reassuring." He adjusted the quilt for maximum coverage.

Emma picked up the spoon and offered him more soup. Although he complained he could do it himself, she ignored his protests and insisted on feeding him like a baby.

She held the spoon in front of him. "May I ask you a question?"

He nodded after swallowing the broth.

"What's a . . ." She paused to reach into her dress pocket and pull out a piece of paper. Smoothing out its creases, she squinted at the paper. "What's a Ferrari?"

A fine spray of soup covered the quilt. "A what?" he sputtered.

"A Ferrari." She dabbed at the material with a towel. "At first, I thought it was a person's name, but you kept talking as if it were more of a something rather than a someone."

"What exactly did I say?"

She tapped her chin. "You said, 'If they take away my Ferrari, I'll never forgive them. I can't live without it.' So . . ." She ladled another spoonful of soup. "What *is* a Ferrari?"

Barrett stared at the spoon, watching the light dance on the surface of the liquid, watching his labored breath make steamy, golden ripples. *That Ferrari was the light of my life . . . until they repossessed it.* For a moment, he remembered the hand-polished canary yellow finish, a beloved weekly chore to fill lonely Sunday mornings. "It's . . . a horse." *Four-hundred horses, to be exact.* The image of the vehicle began to fade, growing unimportant in a world and time where Henry Ford hadn't even built his first car.

"Oh." The answer seemed to satisfy her. She held the spoon to his lips, and he sipped carefully. "Here's the last bit. Would you like me to get you some more? Penny's been keeping a pot of it warm on the stove just for you."

"Uh, no . . . thanks. I think I've had enough."

"You do have to build up your strength. You've had a hard week."

Barrett felt a new bolt of lightning slam into him. "A week? I've been here a week?" He tried to sit up, but she easily pushed him back, evidently a testament to the aforementioned lack of stamina.

"You're in no condition to fight me. You've made me your doctor, so you have to follow my directions."

He settled back to the soft pillow. "I surrender."

"Good." She stood and stretched, letting a small yawn escape.

"When's the last time you ate a good meal and slept in a real bed, Emma?"

"Seems like months." She dropped back to the chair.

"So who takes care of the doctor when the doctor's busy taking care of her patients?"

A bemused smile lit her face. "I like how that sounds."

"What sounds?"

"Her patients."

"That's what I am, aren't I? Your patient?"

She nodded. "I suppose so." The silence drifted like dust in the slanting afternoon sun. After a moment, she leaned toward him. "Johnny . . . may I ask you another question?"

"Uh-huh."

"Why me?"

The sun painted golden highlights in her hair, revealing pale freckles sprinkled across the bridge of her nose. Suddenly the flawless complexions of the women in his day and time seemed as artificial as paint-by-number canvases. "Because . . ."

Because why?

"Because you wouldn't have attempted to operate on me if you thought the barber could honestly have done a better job."

"But, I'm a woman."

"So?"

Soft fingers touched his forehead, and he shifted her hand away.

"I'm not delirious, Emma." He continued to hold her hand, turning it over to display her palm. "I had an aunt who swore she could read palms. I wonder what she would see in yours."

The blush made her freckles stand out even more, but she didn't pull her hand away.

Barrett traced the lines in her palm with his index finger. He wasn't sure, but he thought he felt her tremble a bit. "It says here you will live a very long and very prosperous life."

Her voice stayed remarkably steady. "As a doctor?"

He grinned at her. "I don't see why not."

"You, Mr. Callaghan . . ." She pulled away from him and caught him in a steely stare. "You are what my daddy always called a snake oil salesman." She snatched a bottle from the bedside table and poured out a spoonful of black syrup.

He glared at the unappetizing mixture. "What's that?"

"One of Daddy's home remedies. It'll help the healing process."

Barrett reluctantly accepted the medicine, regretting his decision the moment he tasted the thick, nauseating liquid. "That's supposed to make me better?" he sputtered, recoiling from the bitterness with a shudder.

"My father always said, 'If it doesn't kill you . . . it'll certainly cure you.' "

Barrett clutched his throat, took a couple of gasps, then performed the most spectacularly theatrical death his injuries would allow.

After a moment, she cleared her throat.

"Sheriff, what do you call this . . . this performance?"

Barrett cracked open one eyelid and offered her his most calculated, endearing smile. "Would you believe, *Death of a Snake Oil Salesman?*"

She reached for the bottle of toxic waste again.

"I give up." He started to offer two hands up in surrender but the movement released a freight train of pain to shoot up his side. His next gasp was for real.

Emma pulled down the sheet and examined the bandage swathing his side. "Sheriff, if this wound's bleeding again, you'll drink the whole . . ." She paused, her face tightening in seriousness. ". . . the whole damn bottle!"

Five

Emma watched Johnny's features grow slack as he finally slipped into sleep. Once satisfied that he was comfortable under the effects of the medicine, she tiptoed out of the room and trudged downstairs to the kitchen.

Penny was bent over the stove, retrieving something which smelled heavenly.

"How is he?" The landlady juggled a hot pan with her apron as she stepped from stove to table.

"Ornery as ever." The aroma of the fresh steamy gingerbread made Emma's mouth water. "Even in his sleep."

"Good." Penny nudged the pan toward her. "Help yourself, but be careful. It's hot."

Emma cut herself a generous piece of cake and blew on it until it cooled. As she wolfed it down, she glanced up, feeling a bit like a guilty child caught cutting the Sunday cake.

The woman gave her an indulgent smile. "Now, you're not *that* hungry, are you?"

Penny placed a steaming mug of tea in front of Emma and pushed the sugar bowl closer.

Emma wiped the crumbs from her mouth, then ladled two spoons of sugar into the tea. "Now that I know Johnny's going to be all right, I've rediscovered my appetite. It usually happens like that."

The rickety chair creaked as the landlady sat down. "Just how many patients have you nursed back from the brink of death?"

Emma cut another piece of gingerbread, wondering if Penny meant the words to sound quite so sarcastic. "Too many times to count. In Chattanooga, I was my father's unofficial partner in his practice. Once the patients began to know me, they allowed me to treat their ills when Father was busy or out on a call."

"But why were the two of you willing to leave your home and move out here to Colorado?"

After a moment's reflection, Emma decided the truth was perhaps the best tactic, a truth she wasn't allowed to voice in her hometown. "We ran into some problem with another doctor. One of his most influential patients became unhappy with his care and came to us instead for treatment. The doctor accused us of stealing his patients."

Emma stared at the cake pan, suddenly finding her appetite diminished. "He made it very difficult for us to obtain medicine, and out-and-out lied when we caught a misdiagnosis he performed." She felt a flush of color tinge her cheeks. "You can imagine what terrible things he said about a woman acting as a doctor. Then, someone shot up our dispensary in the middle of the night, and Father decided shortly after that it would be better to move than fight and for me to become a full practicing partner when he arrived here."

"Do you still expect to start a practice here?" Disbelief dripped from every word the woman spoke.

Emma allowed herself a small tight smile, girding up for the usual rhetoric about her inappropriate ideas. "I gather you don't think I can."

Penny tilted her head to one side. "I'm not sure the townspeople will let you."

"But what about Johnny?" Emma thumbed in the direction of the stairs. "*He* let me operate."

The landlady released a rattling sigh. "That one took me by surprise . . . by complete surprise. He's the last person I expected to let you cut into him. I haven't figured that out yet."

Emma started to protest, but Penny cut her off with a gesture.

"Now, honey, I don't mean to slight you in the least. You're a dedicated one, all right. I've watched you tend to him night and day for the better part of a week. You're a good nurse."

"Thanks, Penny." Emma picked at the last crumbs of her gingerbread, wondering how many more years she would have to smile and nod when someone credited her as a dedicated nursemaid rather than a skilled doctor. She heard a cough behind her and turned to see Harvey Kirk filling the doorway.

"Miss Penny, Miss Emma." He nodded affably. "How's . . . the sheriff?"

"Resting comfortably, now."

Harvey played with his watch, reminding Emma of her brother when he had something difficult to say.

"Mr. Kirk, is there something else?"

"Well . . . I . . . uh, I was wondering if I could go upstairs and visit with the sheriff?"

"Normally, I'd say yes, but he's just gone to sleep and I think he needs as much rest as he can get."

"But—"

"Please, Mr. Kirk, he really doesn't need any interruptions. Just let him sleep, and you can come back later."

The man shifted from one foot to the other, then mumbled something which sounded like "Well, you're the doc . . ." as he backed out of the room. Emma looked at

Penny, and they both shrugged simultaneously.

"Odd duck, that Kirk fellow." Penny returned to her stove, stirring a pot of something which smelled even more appetizing than the gingerbread. "Just showed up one day. Don't know where from. He stays away from the whiskey all week except Saturday nights. That man sings the strangest songs when he gets a bellyful of booze. Why, one time he started singing about . . ."

Emma tried to keep her eyes open during Penny's soliloquy, but failed. As she nodded off to sleep, her propped elbow slipped, waking her in time to hear the woman call her name.

"Emma, why don't you go lie down in my room until supper time? You look like you could use the rest."

Sipping the last of her cooled tea, Emma stared out the window into the glint of the late afternoon sun. "I suppose you're right, Penny. Someone has to look after—" *Aw . . . go ahead and say it.* "—the *doctor* as well." Stretching as she rose from the ladder-back chair, she drained her cup, then shuffled toward the stairs.

When Emma trudged up the stairs and entered the landlady's room, an explosion of color took her breath away, bringing her to a gape-mouthed standstill.

Pink gingham covered the room from canopy bed to window seat. Tiny pink bows and ruffled rows of eyelet lace decorated the edges of the curtains. Gold-edged framed pictures of cupids and angels interrupted the symmetry of the candy-striped wallpaper.

Try as she did, Emma couldn't bring herself to recline on the fluffy coverlet, so she chose the window seat instead. Arranging the pillows behind her back, she found a relatively comfortable position and closed her eyes. Shifting, she discovered something hard edging into her spine. The novel she found beneath the pillow appeared wellworn. She opened the book to the page marked with a strip of pink-edged lace.

"Poised in the doorway, the sheik held me captive with his smoldering gaze. Propriety screamed at me, begging me to run from him, but before I could move he strode across the room, fixing me to the cushions with an evil smile.

'Here, woman.' He pointed to a spot at his feet. 'Stand before your master.'

Meekly I took my station.

He stroked my cheek, then his hand dipped lower . . . lower yet, and lower . . . until—"

Emma slammed the book closed and stuffed it beneath the pillow. Hopping from the window seat, she decided to find some other place to rest. *Any* place except Penny's lacy, cushion-strewn boudoir, home of the Sheik and his mesmerized captive.

The threadbare carpet led past Johnny's

room to the stairs. As Emma passed his doorway, she heard voices from his room.

"Here . . . Jeez, be careful, you're spilling the water!"

Emma nudged the door open and watched Harvey Kirk hold a glass of water to Johnny's lips.

"Just one more sip. Not too much. You don't want to spring a leak, do you?"

She stepped into the room, feeling perturbed that her orders had been openly disobeyed. "Mr. Kirk, I thought I asked you not to disturb the sheriff."

The man nearly dropped the glass as he pivoted to face her. "Uh, Miss Emma. I wasn't, I mean, I didn't . . ." He looked down at the tumbler. "I only meant to peek in and see if he was still sleeping. Johnny asked for water and I was just trying to help."

"I was . . . was thirsty." Johnny wiped the water droplets from his chin.

"Well . . ." She stared at the two men, knowing something else was going on between them, but unable to determine exactly what. Johnny seemed no worse for wear, and it *was* important he not become dehydrated. "You can stay . . . for only a few minutes longer." She switched her glare from the guilty-looking Mr. Kirk to the equally guilty-looking sheriff. "That is if Johnny doesn't mind."

The odd man raised his hand and gestured with a surprisingly well-manicured hand, drawing a cross over his heart. "Just five minutes, Miss Nolan. I promise."

Harvey waited until Emma closed the door before he spoke again. "I thought for a moment there she'd seen the pill bottle." He reached into his pocket and pulled out the plastic vial. "It says to take one every four hours." He handed Barrett the bottle.

"Thank God for modern medicines." Barrett hid the container beneath the covers. "Are you sure they don't have antibiotics in this century?"

"I checked. Apparently Pasteur started playing around with them fifteen years earlier, but nothing substantial happens until Fleming stumbles onto penicillin in the 1920s."

"Well, I plan to be long gone from here before then." Barrett grimaced as he shifted in the bed. "Do you have anything for the pain? I feel like my side's on fire."

Harvey fished out his watch and probed its darkened face. "You ought to be thankful I happen to have these antibiotics left from that unfortunate incident with the Roman gladiator." He grimaced. "Lessee . . . all I have left is some aspirin. I can get you something stronger on Saturday when I go back."

"If I live that long."

"I know that feeling. May I?" Harvey gestured at the bandage. "I've seen my share of gunshot wounds."

Barrett nodded, and shifted so the man could peel back the gauze and examine the injury.

"You know what? She did a pretty good job. I've seen in-the-field operations by military doctors that didn't look this neat."

"In the field? Where? Desert Storm?"

Harvey shot him a hooded glance and hesitated before he spoke. "Uh . . . yeah. The Gulf. Anyways . . ." He tried to smile. "Miss Nolan has definitely found her calling." He repositioned the bandage, wincing in sympathy as Barrett reacted to the painful sensation. "Sorry." Harvey uncapped the aspirin vial and shook out two tablets, offering them to Barrett. "Unfortunately, this isn't quite the right time for her to make a living as a surgeon."

Barrett sat up as much as he could to accept the aspirin and the water. "Oh c'mon, Harvey. There've got to be other female doctors in the world around this time period."

"I suppose there are. But they're probably in major metropolitan areas like New York or Philadelphia, not two-bit mining towns in the heart of the Rockies." Harvey helped Barrett lean back on the pillow. "Now you just stay here and let the medicine do its work. Okay?"

Barrett surrendered to the sudden fatigue

which made him close his eyes. "Just as long as you promise I'll wake up . . ."

He slept, dreaming of the piece of paper which would change his life. The property deed. Then, his dreams turned to what that new life would be. He envisioned himself back in his cherished Ferrari with the ravishing Angela gracefully draping the passenger's seat. She would give him looks of awe, mixed with unbridled passion.

Then she would . . . she would . . .

. . . change into Emma.

Barrett awoke and sat straight up, remembering his injury only moments before the inferno of pain rekindled. He clamped his jaw shut rather than release a few of the more inventive combinations of cuss words he'd learned from the mine foreman.

Barrett had learned most of the words during the ten agonizing minutes he'd suffered at the bottom of the mine shaft. It was supposed to be an above-ground summer job at the Daisy Lee, but Barrett had been bullied and shamed into trying to go underground. Once he stepped off the elevator, his fears hit him full force. When the foreman realized the full and true extent of the boss son's claustrophobia, Barrett learned a whole new vocabulary.

Now, as the pain rocked through him, he found he couldn't draw a deep enough breath to utter a single expletive. He remembered to breathe only after he resettled to the pillow. A soft noise drew his attention to the chair beside the bed. Somehow, it didn't surprise him to see Emma there, stationed next to him.

Moonlight from the window painted silvery shadows across her serene face. It wasn't as much her beauty, but the character in her expression, which riveted his gaze. And with Emma asleep, he felt no guilt about staring at her, trying to determine what, when, how she'd come to enter his dreams.

Up to now, Angela had filled his fantasies, Angela, the Untouchable Ice Queen who snubbed his advances and fueled even more dreams with her cold rejection.

But Emma?

Why?

Barrett had no intention of staying in the past. Once he changed the course of history, he intended to reemerge in his own rightful time, reveling in a life of new prosperity. No federal warrants, no looks of pity mixed with disappointment from dismissed employees, no vice presidents living it up in Rio spending the company's hard-earned money on good booze and bad broads.

Callan Industries would be healthy and happy with Barrett Callan at the helm.

That was . . . if he could keep the land out of Thornwald's hands.

Thornwald!

In the haste to fit in as Johnny, Barrett had forgotten the first rule of corporate takeovers: Know thine enemy. And he'd neglected that very important preliminary step. *As soon as I get out of here, I've got to start investigating this Thornwald person.*

His gaze settled on Emma, who was curled up in the chair with a quilt tucked beneath her chin.

Men with a mission didn't have time for pleasure.

He turned away and watched the moonlight stream in through the window. A man from the future didn't have time to romance a woman from the past. The women in this day and age were different from those of his time period.

As different as night and day.

Barrett glanced into the darkened sky, spotting a familiar constellation. *Orion.* He smiled in spite of himself, and closed his eyes.

Not *everything* would be different, a century into the future.

The next morning, he awoke feeling stiff, sore, and alone. Emma had abandoned her post sometime during the night. The sharp pain in his side had dulled to an aching throb. For the first time in a few days, he felt ravenous. But even worse, he felt the call of nature. Now he was glad Emma had left.

The first hurdle: sitting up. The room remained remarkably stable as he shifted his legs to the edge of the bed. He braced himself against the bedside table as he stood. The towel which had been draped across his waist fell to the floor. He ignored the sudden, cool discomfort, determined not to pass out . . . naked.

Barrett lurched to the washstand and held on for dear life. After a few thudding heartbeats, he released one hand to dip in the basin of water and splash his face. Dragging his gaze up to the mirror, he barely recognized himself.

The "Miami Vice" look didn't work on him. Never had. He looked terrible with a fledgling beard. Now it was coupled with pale, near-bloodless features with the exception of the dark circles beneath his eyes. He stared at his reflection. "Johnny, I hope you appreciate what I've gone through for you."

Johnny didn't say anything.

Barrett heard a knock at the door.

"Sheriff . . . you awake?"

Miss Penny!

Barrett glanced down at his nakedness.

He stumbled toward the bed, unable to bend over and retrieve the towel on the floor. Instead, he slipped under the covers with minimum difficulties before the landlady trooped into the room.

"And how are *we*, today?" She balanced a tray in one hand and primped her too-perfect curls with the other. Her dress reminded Barrett of a peppermint nightmare: red and pink with white lace, and constructed with enough material to make a couple of parachutes.

He managed a halfhearted smile. "We're feeling much better, thank you. Uh . . . where's—" He caught himself before he used 'Emma.' "—Miss Nolan?"

Penny hooked her foot around the chair and pulled it closer to the bed. "Emma knew she could rely on me to take good care of *our* patient. I've brought you some oatmeal for breakfast. We have to build up our strength, you know." Somehow she managed to perch the tray across the rolls of flesh which occupied the place where her lap should be. Odd lights danced in her eyes, almost turning her expression into a hungry leer. She reached over to the night stand and snared the bottle of black draught.

Barrett's stomach turned at the memory of the brew's evil stench and revolting taste.

"But first, you've got to take your medicine!" She reached into her pocket and pulled out a spoon the size of a tennis racket. Before Barrett could protest, she measured out a pint of witches' brew and shoved it in his face. "Medicine, then breakfast."

His stomach screamed its surrender, begging for the release of the hostage-held breakfast. Barrett gave in, reluctantly accepting the tarry syrup. He nearly gagged.

Miss Penny graced him with a beatific smile, ladled a spoon of lumpy mush, and waved it under his nose. "Now, open up like a good boy."

Barrett suddenly recognized her look of hunger, realizing it had nothing to do with food. He sat up and took the spoon from her. "Uh . . . thanks, but I can feed myself." He became suddenly self-conscious of his bared chest and tugged the blanket up.

The look of expectancy dried up on her face. "Are you sure?" she asked in a dejected voice.

"Positive." He shoveled the oatmeal in, realizing taste didn't matter at the moment. At least hunger was one pain he could control and eventually eliminate.

The "more than maternal" smile returned again. "My goodness! A big strong man like you gone so long without sustenance . . . no wonder you're *hungry*." She emphasized the word, highlighting too many meanings for an injured man to ponder.

He answered with a nod and waited until he swallowed before speaking. "F-famished. Where did you say Miss Nolan was?"

Penny released a sigh. "At school. The town council was getting upset at her for shirking her teaching duties while she tended to you."

He spoke between mouthfuls. "Looks like

the town council would be thrilled to discover they have a real doctor in their midst."

"A *real* doctor?" Penny's rolls of fat began to jiggle as she laughed. She placed a meaty hand on his forehead. "Are you starting to run a fever again, Sheriff?"

"The Look" had served him well through some of the more trying times in several twentieth-century boardrooms. Everyone from janitors to corporate presidents had been known to be rendered near speechless after receiving "The Look." Barrett discovered it worked just as well in this century as he turned it in Miss Penny's direction.

She flushed, the color deepening as it traveled from her ample cleavage up to her face, which suddenly matched her dress. "I-I better let you eat. If you need anything . . ." She reached into her apron pocket and pulled out a small bell, which she tossed on the bedside table. Hurrying out of the room, she reminded Barrett of a big red thundercloud.

Red sky at morning, sailor take warning.

Lord help him if she ever decided to make a midnight visit to check on his health.

Red sky at night would be no sailor's delight.

He dug into the bowl of mush, scraping the sides to get every last morsel. The coffee had cooled a bit, but the bowl of muffins had been wrapped up in a towel which had kept them steamy hot. He polished off the breakfast, then gingerly tried standing again. This time, his strength didn't ebb quite as much as before. He met the call to nature in the chamber pot, then decided to get dressed.

Barrett managed to balance on the edge of the bed and pull on the long johns. He discovered that, by rolling the waist down a bit, he could avoid putting pressure on the bandage. Although curiosity whispered for him to take a look at Emma's surgical handiwork, he resisted the temptation to peek beneath the gauze.

Blood and gore had never been his strong suit.

He sat on the bed, only wanting to catch his breath before he dressed any further, but exhaustion combined with the intoxicating warmth of the sun wove a spell around him and lulled him back to sleep.

Before she left the schoolroom, Emma gave Ford a list of chores which included a few extra responsibilities designed as punishment for his dangerous foolishness. She carried her books up to Johnny's room, planning to grade some students' papers as she sat with her patient. But once she found her magazine hiding among the schoolwork, she decided to shirk her duty for a little recreational reading.

Absorbed in the story, she failed to notice her patient until he spoke.

"Whatcha reading?"

She looked up, startled by his deep voice. "You're awake."

"What are you reading?" he repeated, his words fuzzed with sleep.

"It's a story called 'A Scandal in Bohemia.'"

"Sherlock Holmes?"

The extra beat of her heart betrayed her surprise. "You're familiar with the story?"

"Uh-huh." He yawned. "That's the one with Irene Adler and the compromising photograph of the King of Bohemia, right?"

She stared at the magazine in her hands. "Y-yes." *How could he know about this?*

A sleepy smile lightened his face. "Ah yes . . . how does it start? Something about Holmes always referring to her as *the* woman'? The only person besides Moriarty who could outsmart the great detective?"

"Who?"

"The world's greatest detective. Sherlock Holmes."

She stared at him. "No, I mean Moriarty. Who's Moriarty?"

"Professor James Moriarty. Holmes's arch enemy. Remember their death struggle at the brink of Reichenbach Falls? Everyone thought Sherlock was a goner, 'specially poor Dr. Watson. Turns out the author had merely grown tired of the emen . . . mimnenable, nemi-mable . . ." He paused to make a face. ". . . of good ol' Sherlock and decided to kill him off, but the reading public wouldn't stand for it. No sireebob!"

She realized his words weren't merely fuzzy with sleep, but slurred as if he were drunk. Emma put down her magazine and crossed to his bed to check his temperature. His skin was pleasantly cool to the touch. She couldn't blame his odd manner on a fever. Turning, she suddenly caught sight of Johnny's draught mixture.

He released a laugh wrapped in a cloud of whiskey. "Yep, I even tried to find 221B Baker Street when I was in London a couple of years ago."

She held up the bottle, revealing only a few drops of black syrup coating the bottom of the glass. "Johnny, did you take your medicine today?"

"Of course I did. Just as the doctor ordered. And Miz Penny made me some mighty fine coffee today. Drank lots and lots of that. Don't want to get dee-hydrated, you know. Poor woman . . . dehydration seemed to be a concept she couldn't quite fathom." He giggled. "Get it? Dehydration . . . *fathom!* Aquatic humor!"

Emma picked up his empty coffee cup and sniffed at the dregs. More whiskey than coffee grounds. *Penny!* The medicine was half alcohol as it was, but combined with generous nips of liquor in each coffee cup, it was no wonder he was drunk. Of course, the pain he lacked today would double tomorrow as he coped with his healing gunshot wound *and* a hangover.

But his ravings about Sherlock Holmes. She'd never met a man who developed such a fertile imagination when drunk. Pink elephants and dancing bears, yes. But Sherlock Holmes? Where had he even heard of the Great Detective? She probably had the only copy of the *Strand* magazine between Denver and San Francisco. And she knew for a fact that Johnny had never stepped a foot out of Colorado. He'd told her so himself when they first met.

"Why so sad, Doctor Watson?" He reached up for her hand, capturing it in a loose grasp.

"You're drunk."

"Nonsense." He began to play with her fingers, caressing them with light strokes. "Haven't had a drink all day, 'cept coffee." He pressed her hand to his lips, sending a shivery but pleasant feeling up her arm. "You know there are some theories afoot that Watson was a woman."

For one brief moment, she didn't want to move. She wanted Johnny Callaghan to hold her hand and smile at her. And if he had to be drunk in order to do so, she didn't care.

"Was the good doctor a lady? Inquiring minds want to know."

She looked down at his crooked grin, then jerked her hand away.

She cared, all right. She wanted Johnny fully conscious and cognizant of his actions when he held her hand. She wanted to know the words came from the man, not from the alcohol. She wanted that perfect white smile all for herself.

Perfect . . .

His grin widened. "Whatcha looking at?"

She turned her head away. "Nothing."

"Oh c'mon . . . tell me."

She hesitated for a moment, then shrugged away her reservations. He probably wouldn't even remember this tomorrow. "Your smile. I didn't remember you had such . . ." What could she say? Perfect teeth? ". . . such a nice smile."

"Should be nice." He closed his eyes, but the grin remained. "My parents spent a fortune getting my teeth straightened when I was a kid." His voice began to fade and his words to falter. "Dad said *he* paid enough to put the orthodontist's son through college. I had a couple of classes with the kid and I can tell you one thing." His grin faded. "The money was wasted on him. He was no rocket scientist."

Emma couldn't help but stare at him. *Orthodontist? Rocket scientist?*

She had difficulty swallowing.
The man shouldn't be reading fiction.
He should be writing it!

Six

Barrett decided to be up and dressed before Emma arrived for his morning checkup. As he struggled with the button fly of his pants, he wondered why men in the future had revived such an archaic and time-consuming fashion. *I wonder when the zipper was invented* . . .

He heard a knock at the door.

"Sheriff?" Emma's soft voice barely penetrated the door.

"Come in."

She entered, took one look at his bare chest, and backed into the door frame, blushing furiously. "I'll w-wait outside until you're done."

He gestured for her to come in. "Don't go, Emma. It's not as if you haven't seen me without a shirt before." He stared down at the recalcitrant buttons, his vision blurring for a moment. His balance wavered, and he reached out to steady himself, hoping she hadn't noticed, but she stepped toward him. Soft kid leather gloves touched his skin, helping to brace him. He hated the leather, which added an impersonal barrier to a warm touch he'd gotten used to.

"Dizzy?" Her blush faded into a look of concern.

Barrett knew that if he nodded, the room just might spin off in another direction. "It's not as much dizzy as . . ." He waved off her help, hesitating before voicing the words. ". . . feeling as if I were hung over."

Her grin caught Barrett by surprise. When she seemed to realize he was staring at her, she covered her giggle with her gloved hand. "Please, Sheriff . . . I'm not laughing at you. Honestly."

Barrett stiffened, waiting to see which stopped its revolutions first, the room, his head, or his stomach. He released a deep breath only after the room skidded to a jarring halt.

"Sheriff?" Emma stripped off her glove and reached for his elbow. Her touch was warm, reassuring. "Don't you think you ought to sit down?"

The moment after he shook his head, Barrett braced himself for an onslaught of gyrations, but the room remained remarkably still. "I-I feel all right." He tried to smile. "I really do," he added when she gave him a look of undisguised suspicion. "I have a job to do, Emma, and I can't do it from here." *I won't be able to find out anything about*

Thornwald if I'm holed up here, playing patient. He rubbed at the irritating absence on his finger where his ring used to reside.

She pulled off her grey cloak and tossed it toward the chair, then balanced her fists on her calico-clad hips. Her relative height increased as her face grew more stern. "And you think you'll be able to make your rounds as usual despite the fact that you almost died only a week ago?"

"Emma . . . I promise to sit at my desk and delegate my authority. I'll let Jimmie and a couple of the temporary deputies handle everything. I'll just coordinate."

She stared at him. "Coordinate? And delegate?" She shook her head, then gestured to his bandage. "Let me check that before you put on your shirt." She examined his wound with the clinical air of an HMO professional, speaking in grunts instead of words.

He looked down and addressed the top of her head. "Is 'Hrummpt' good or bad?"

"Good . . . this time." She expertly applied a new bandage, surprising him with the gentleness of her touch, offset by the doubt on her face. He prayed that an endearing expression would charm her away from her growing suspicions. He gave her his most disarming grin. "Uh . . . could you hand me my shirt?"

Emma gave him one more pointed "I-know-something's-wrong-but-I-don't-know-what-it-is" glare, then retrieved the garment. She remained quiet as he buttoned the shirt.

Before he could say anything, she picked up his vest, fingering the puckered seam which marred its side. "Penny did the best repair job she could with your vest."

Barrett couldn't maintain his smile as he tried to ignore the hole which neatly corresponded with the bandage hiding beneath his shirt. "Maybe she can make me a bulletproof vest next time." The moment the words escaped his lips, he felt like kicking himself. *Bulletproof? You idiot. One more crack like that and it's a one-way ticket to the nearest loony bin!*

But Emma merely nodded. "I bet you wished you'd been wearing a vest of chain mail instead of leather. That certainly would have stopped the bullet." Her face darkened. "But if it hadn't been for me, you wouldn't have been shot to begin with."

"Emma." The aggravation began to build in him. "Would you please can the guilt-trip speech?"

She stared at him, confusion paling her features. "The what? I don't understand what in the world you are talking about, Sheriff."

"The guilt-trip . . . er . . . trying to shoulder all the blame yourself. It was my job to protect the townspeople, and that's all I was doing."

"But I should have—"

He placed a finger across her lips. "I told you. It wasn't your fault."

The moment he touched her, a flush started to color her cheeks. She stepped back from his gesture at the same time he did. "Well . . . I need to get to school and prepare for my students. I'll let you go to work, Sheriff Callaghan, if you promise me you'll stay at your desk and . . . *delegate* your *authority* from there." She placed emphasis on the two words, making Barrett wonder how badly he'd betrayed himself.

"I promise. And please, after all we've been through, it's . . . Johnny."

"J-Johnny . . ." She stuttered his name, wearing a strained smile. Despite the speed of her exit, her skirts almost caught in the door which slammed behind her.

Barrett tried to fasten the holster at his waist, but the gun's weight put too much pressure on his bandage. Looping the holster over one shoulder, he took a deep breath and followed in Emma's lavender-scented wake. But the counter-aroma of breakfast grew overpowering, and Barrett allowed his stomach to control the navigation. It led him to Miss Penny's sideboard, which was laden with enough food to feed the Seventh Fleet.

She clucked over him like a bride serving her bridegroom their first meal. Her fawning

care unnerved him, and Barrett bolted
through his eggs and bacon at breakneck
speed. Recharged, he made it to his office
before exhaustion placed dark specks in his
vision. Easing himself into the desk chair, he
took a deep breath before reaching for the
stack of notes impaled on an upturned nail
which was evidently the nineteenth-century
version of an answering machine. He fanned
out the notes across his desk.

Jailed Harvey from Sat. night to Mon. morn.
Drunk.

Sunday morn.—cleanup detail. Silas in charge.

The Hanleys fighting again. She hit him w/
iron skillet, so jailed Ralph to keep him out of
range Wed. after church social.

Rec'd telegram from federal marshal about bank
holdup in ColoSpgs. Suspect robbers may be from
Kansas City. Fri. morn.

Rec'd Wanted posters. Fri. morn.

Jailed Harvey from Sat. night to Mon. morn.
Drunk.

Spousal abuse, alcohol abuse, armed rob-
bery . . . *Crime is crime, no matter what the*
century. Nothing's changed.

He heard the footfalls on the wooden porch before the door even opened.

". . . and I told him that—Sheriff!" Jimmie Soames gaped at Barrett, while the deputy's companion cast a disinterested glance in Johnny's direction. "Good God Almighty, I didn't expect to see you up and around so soon, Johnny." His shocked expression transformed into a genuine smile. "I always thought you was a tough sumbitch."

The other man stepped forward, wearing no smile, genuine or otherwise. "Thank God you've returned to your duties, Sheriff. I thought I was going to have to deal with your subordinate, here. What are you going to do about this?" He slapped a piece of paper on the desk.

Barrett recognized it as a telegram about the bank robberies. "Well . . ." He scratched his chin, stalling for time.

The man crossed his arms. "It's your duty to protect my bank and I want to know exactly how you intend on doing that."

Your bank? The light dawned. *Thornwald!* The mountain had come to Mohammed. The pain in Barrett's side began to fade as his mind sharpened. "Well first, I want to review your security precautions. Examine your internal procedures and run through a few scenarios to ascertain the effectiveness of your defenses. Then we can identify any weaknesses and repair the disparities in the bank's protection."

Jimmie gaped at him with dumbfounded amazement.

Thornwald's look of astonishment dissolved to a raised-eyebrow agreement. "You surprise me, Sheriff. I think we speak the same language." His growing smile oozed assurance.

The deputy turned his glazed stare toward the banker. "You understood what he said?" he asked in hushed reverence.

Thornwald ignored Jimmie. "When do you propose to make this review of our safeguards?"

"What about this afternoon? Quite frankly, I need to gauge my energy. Not too much in reserve at the moment, but I foresee it as merely a temporary inconvenience."

"Of course, Sheriff Callaghan. I understand." The man consulted the watch he pulled out of his waistcoat pocket. "Shall we say two o'clock? At the bank?"

"Two o'clock, then."

Thornwald took a step toward the door, then stopped, pivoting to face Barrett. "Sheriff, I know our paths haven't crossed much since I moved here last spring, but I must say it's a surprise to find a man of your evident intelligence here . . ." He stopped to indicate the barren office with a careless gesture. ". . . in such a position."

Barrett balanced his smile with a shrug. "People will surprise you, Mr. Thornwald. It's the nature of a capricious humanity. Good day, sir."

As the banker moved toward the door, Jimmie made no pretense of hiding his stunned expression. "Where . . . how . . ." He took off his hat and swiped his brow with his flanneled arm. "I've never heard so many fancy two-dollar words in all my born days. And half of 'em were from you!" Jimmie dropped into the chair beside the desk. "I sat beside you in the schoolroom 'til we were both thirteen years old and I know you never learned them there. What did Miz Emma do? Pour in some learnin' while she had you opened up on the operating table?"

Barrett's pains returned as the adrenaline levels faded. He always operated best under pressure, and facing Thornwald was definitely a stress builder. But now he had a new problem. "Well, Jimmie, I've been hitting the books some. You know, reading. I guess I just picked up some of those words from there. Sort of by osmosis."

"Os . . . os—what?"

Dig the pit a bit deeper, why doncha? "Never mind." He pointed to the slips of paper spread out over his desk. "Anything else other than these problems you need to tell me about?"

"That's pretty much all of it. But I still

wish you'd let me throw the book at McConnell."

"Who?"

"McConnell, the miner who shot you. I think it might do him a world of good. Even his mates think he ought to do a little hard labor on this one."

"What about making him do some community service?"

"You mean making him do something for the town?" Jimmie got up and shuffled over to the stove, where a black pot steamed peacefully. He poured a noxious-looking brew into a tin cup and gestured with the pot to Barrett. "Want some?" At the negative answer, Jimmie returned, gingerly nursing the hot coffee. "I like the idea of making him pay for the damages he caused. Just might make him think twice about wearing a gun when he knows he's aiming to get drunker'n a skunk. Anyways, he's got time on his hands 'cause he got suspended from his job for two weeks. What d'ya think he ought to do to make it up to you and the town?"

Barrett concentrated past the lightning bolts in his side, trying to envision a suitably demeaning task for the man who shot him. But how much more demeaning could it be than to work underground in a tiny passage?

In the dark.

With the walls closing in on you.

And a thousand tons of rock and dirt overhead held from crashing in on you by only a couple of wooden braces . . .

He began to sweat, his breath coming in short gasps. The shreds of fear began to congeal, to grow, pressing on him like the imaginary walls of the mine shafts he'd learned to avoid a long time ago. For a moment, the pain and the fear intermingled, becoming one. Then slowly he separated them, the fear imaginary, the pain all too real. After a few labored breaths, he regained control, suddenly cognizant of Jimmie's frantic voice.

". . . just stay there, I'll go get Miz Emma. She'll know what to do."

"No." Barrett spoke in a rasp. "No," he repeated more firmly, "I'll be okay, now. It was just a momentary twinge." He managed a wincing smile. "It's all right now. See?"

"Well . . . I don't know. You went awfully pale and I thought you was going to pass out or somethin'."

"I'll just sit here and do some paperwork. You handle the foot patrols and any drunken, armed rioters. Okay?"

Jimmie beamed, evidently his worst fears assuaged by Barrett's forced humor. The deputy rifled through the files anchoring one end of the desk and pulled out a sheaf of papers. "Here're the latest Wanted posters. I thought you'd like to look them over before I put them up."

The blurry faces all looked identically stiff, reminding Barrett how his view of the past had been no more substantial than a chapter in a history book. But the faces of the people he'd met since he traveled back in time bore no resemblance to the frozen photographs in the texts forced upon him in high school and college. History had been a necessary evil on the road to a degree, but now history was no longer merely a subject taught to an unwilling student; history was alive, populated by real people with lives, families, even distinctive personalities.

"Ugly-looking lot." Barrett shuffled the papers into a neat stack.

Jimmie nodded. "You say that every time."

Barrett did a double take. "I do?"

"Yep. And then you always suggest I post them near the cells to scare the rats away."

"R-rats?" Barrett glanced down beneath the desk. "I haven't noticed any rats."

The deputy chuckled as he scooped up the papers. "Just goes to show you how well the posters work."

A familiar shiver trooped up Barrett's spine. *Aw . . . Rats.*

The soft scratch of chalk filled the schoolroom.

"The next word is *journey*. 'He took a long journey to visit a place where he had never gone before.'"

"Where, Miz Emma?" Beth Angley wiped her nose on her sleeve, depositing a smear of chalk dust across her face.

"What do you mean, Beth?"

"Where did the man go?"

"Sweetheart, this isn't a story. It's a spelling test."

"Oh." The little girl stared down at her chalkboard and made a few tentative marks, then looked up again with doe-eyes. "Will you tell us where he went *after* we finish the spelling test?"

Emma kept her laughter to herself, knowing the fragile child wouldn't understand the source of her teacher's reaction. "Yes, Beth, we'll have story time after recess and I'll tell you where he went. All right children, the last word is *travel*. 'I want to travel all the way to . . .'" She searched for a suitable destination. "'. . . to Pittsburgh.'" *Now where did I get that from?* A second later, she remembered Johnny's words about flying to Pittsburgh. She gave herself a mental shake.

"It's time for recess, so leave your slates on your desks and I'll grade your tests. Walk!" she admonished as some of her more exuberant students leapt toward the door. Emma picked up the first slate, knowing every word would be spelled correctly. The

Pamplin boy was a star student, smart, eager to learn, and blessed with parents who valued his education. It was the combination of all three things which made him shine in the class. Many of her other students lacked one ingredient of the key mixture to really excel in school.

Had Johnny Callaghan been a star student as well?

When he first introduced himself, he'd seemed pleasantly taciturn, measuring his words with a cautious smile. Emma smiled in spite of herself, remembering how he helped her down from the stagecoach and steadied her as she regained her "land" legs after such a long trip over the treacherous mountain curves. She'd fallen for him two seconds after she'd met him, and so, she found out later, had every other eligible and not-so-eligible female in town.

The first time Emma saw the sheriff in what she deemed "heroic action," her infatuation grew to embarrassing proportions, which made it necessary to avoid him as much as possible. Being the schoolmistress had its rank and privileges, but there was also a stigma to being unwed in a town where the only single females were either under thirteen, or ladies of the evening. Every unattached male in town thought she was fair game and they inundated her with gifts right after her arrival. Every man, that was, but Johnny Callaghan, who seemed very content—even admired by the lesser mortals—with his unattached status.

Here, she was considered a spinster, with all its unattractive connotations, while he was called a bachelor, a man who cherished his freedom. It served as yet another example of the inequality between the sexes.

Emma glanced at the slate in her hands and read the childish scrawl.

Trip. Remote. Conductor. Wagon. Engine. Suitcase. Ticket. Continent. Journey. Travel. Remote . . .

Johnny had used it as a noun, not as a description of an isolated location. *"Where's the remote?"* he had said while he thrashed around in his delirium, evidently looking for an object.

A whoop, bellow, and crash interrupted her thoughts. A minute later Emma had two playground miscreants standing in opposite corners of the schoolroom, and she returned to the task of grading the spelling slates.

School lagged more for the teacher than the students that day. For some reason, Emma had an irritating itch of curiosity which refused to respond to the balm of logic. Following in the wake of the last child who straggled out of the schoolroom, Emma headed over to the sheriff's office to check on her recovering patient.

Once there, she hesitated for a brief moment as she stood on the sidewalk. Most men didn't like to be reminded of their frailties in front of anyone, especially other men. If the deputy or others were there, she would have to gauge her words carefully.

The games we play . . .

"Sheriff?" Emma stepped into the office. A pot of coffee steamed on the potbellied stove but no one was in sight. *Maybe he's gone back to rest.*

Although she felt a bit silly, Emma took the back steps to the boarding house, hoping to avoid Penny. Over the course of their week together, Emma had learned to appreciate the woman's cooking talents and ability to face some of the less appealing chores of dealing with the sick, but Emma also learned to fear Penny's "helpful" suggestions, which many times turned out to be a horrible conglomeration of old wives' tales involving weird chants, chicken feathers, and the burying of personal articles in the dead of night.

Once upstairs unobserved, Emma knocked lightly on his door, wondering if he had spent his meager reserves of energy and was asleep.

"Johnny?" she called softly.

There was no answer.

She turned the knob and peeked in. No one home.

A thunderous charge of footfalls echoed

down the hallway. A feminine hum filled the air.

Penny!

Emma slipped into Johnny's room, closed the door, and held her breath. The stampede proceeded down the hallway without stopping, then disappeared down the back steps. Emma released her breath with a relieved sigh, jumping only when she caught unexpected sight of her reflection in the mirror. Her surprise faded to a guilt-choked smile.

You're acting so silly.

She dipped her fingers in the china basin and splashed a little water on her face. Reaching for a towel, she found none on the washstand. She automatically reached into the drawer, having learned they were stored there during her role as Johnny's doctor. As she pulled out the last towel, a metallic clink sounded at her feet. She saw a flash of white disappear beneath the washstand.

Hastily wiping her face, Emma stooped to peer beneath the oak stand, and spotted a wad of newspaper resting between gigantic dust balls. She batted the object out of its hiding place and gingerly held it between her thumb and forefinger.

Curiosity overcame her. The newspaper wrapping came undone without tearing.

The gold ring weighed heavily in her palm, the red stone winking as it caught the sun. Letters formed a circle around the stone. "Harvard University." Emma's mouth dropped open. The engraving on one side of the ring read " '85" and on the other side, "BA." Her throat began to tighten.

This can't be his ring. She held it up to the light to view the engraving on the inside of the ring.

JBC V, June 1, 1885.

She blinked.

No. It said, *June 1, 1985.*

Seven

Her hand remained remarkably steady as logic rushed in to bridge the gaps in her understanding.

The ring . . . was it Johnny's? No, she told herself. It belonged to somebody else.

The engraving was . . . a mistake. Even better, it was someone's idea of a practical joke.

But what about the conspicuous groove on his finger? There was only one obvious answer; he wore another ring which he had recently stopped wearing. Or lost. It was so simple.

Emma glanced at the initials again. *JBC V.* Her treacherous thoughts formed before she could stop them. John B. Callaghan. Her mind stuttered over the "V." There was a space between the third and fourth initials. The obvious answer made the "1985" become eerily possible. *John B. Callaghan, the Fifth.*

After a moment's thought, she smoothed out the newspaper; it was last week's *Margin*

Gazette. Angry that it didn't substantiate her wild theory, she twisted the paper savagely around the ring. Her hands lost their steadiness as she shoved the wrapped package back beneath the hastily folded towel. She closed the drawer, stepped back, and stared at the offensive washstand.

The words of the Master Detective rang in her mind. *"When you have eliminated the impossible, whatever remains, however improbable, must be the truth."*

What was impossible?

1985?

No, barring Armageddon, 1985 was a probable future, albeit a distant one.

Harvard University. That was a reality. It would likely exist a hundred years from now as it has existed a hundred years ago.

Time travel?

She remembered marveling over Mr. Verne's novel *Mysterious Island,* but she never seriously considered the possible reality of time travel.

Emma took a few stumbling steps back and sat down hard on Johnny's bed. What was she trying to tell herself? That Johnny had traveled into the future? That he had pretended to be his own . . . ancestor, had received an education at Harvard and returned, fully matriculated but lacking the skills he once had as sheriff?

And all of this overnight? He certainly

hadn't taken any mysterious trips since she'd moved there. And it all seemed to start the day he gave Ford the silver dollar by mistake.

Her heart began to thunder, the rhythm jumping to an almost unbearable tempo when she heard footfalls on the stairs. When the door swung open, she squeezed her eyes shut like a child saying, "If I can't see you, you can't see me."

"Emma?"

She opened her eyes in reluctance and spotted the bedraggled Johnny Callaghan standing in the doorway. His clothes hung off him, indicating how much weight he'd lost during his recuperation. She noticed his alarming lack of color and the beads of sweat on his upper lip.

He moved with surprising speed to the foot of the bed. "Are you all right? You look like you've seen a ghost!" Johnny reached out to touch her, but she couldn't stop herself from shrinking away.

"No . . ." She wasn't sure whether she was telling him not to touch her, or that she didn't believe the fantastic thoughts which whirled around her head.

"What's wrong?" He sagged against the bedpost, clutching it with whitened knuckles.

Emma drew a deep breath. "Sit." She watched him grimace as he lowered to the feather mattress. Johnny closed his eyes and muttered something about "overdoing it." He winced as he stretched out.

The ring and its implications faded as she became a doctor again, measuring his temperature and pulse. Although both seemed normal, she decided to check his bandage anyway and assure herself there had been no resurgence of infection.

As she started to unbutton his shirt, he cracked open one eye. "I've never had a doctor make a house call *before* I even called her."

The pale flash of his perfect smile made the maelstrom of questions return. Emma took a moment to gird her resolve, then retrieved the ring from the washstand drawer.

"Can you explain this?"

He stared at the newspaper-wrapped object resting in the center of her palm. "I . . . uh . . . I mean . . ." He stopped, then turned his stare to her. "How the hell did you find that?" Johnny pushed up cautiously on one elbow. "You were searching through my things, weren't you? You had no—" A spasm of pain flashed across his face, choking off his protests.

"Just calm down, Johnny." She helped him settle back to the pillow.

"I'm calm," he said from between clenched teeth. "Just give it to me." He tried to take the ring from her hand, but she tightened her grasp.

"No, you tell me about this thing. Why does it say nineteen eighty-five instead of eighteen eighty-five? Why does it have your initials on it? And what does the 'V' mean?"

He said nothing, but his pale expression screamed duplicity.

She felt her world slowly closing in on itself. "Johnny, you have to tell me . . . please. Is this what I think it is?"

He tried to smile, but the expression slipped away quickly. He wrapped one hand around his ribs and closed his eyes again. "The future."

Emma thought she heard him wrong. "The what?"

"The future. The ring's from the future."

She opened her fingers and stared at the bit of gold peeking out of the torn newspaper. "Then it *is* from nineteen eighty-five. But how? How did you get it? How do you know it's not just a joke?"

Anticipation and silence built to a roar in her ears.

Finally, he spoke.

"Because it's mine."

Barrett refused to open his eyes. Perhaps he could put off the inevitable by playing possum. If she thought he had passed out or was asleep or—

"You're from nineteen eighty-five?" It wasn't disbelief dripping from her voice, as much as awe. "Nineteen eighty-five . . ." she repeated in a faded voice.

"No." Barrett kept his eyes shut. "I'm not from nineteen eighty-five. That's just when I graduated from Harvard. I'm from nineteen ninety-five."

It sounded like a giggle.

Then it grew.

Barrett cracked one eye open and saw the smile beneath the camouflage of her hands. He braced himself for an onslaught of hysterics, but her laughter seemed more relieved than on the edge of panic and confusion.

"Oh, thank God." She released her deep breath in a quick explosion. "I was afraid I was going crazy or something." She folded her hands into a tense knot like a child straining to prove her patience.

"You . . . crazy?" Barrett managed to sit up in spite of the fatigue which had turned his muscles to mush. "Aren't you supposed to accuse *me* of being crazy?"

Her gaze narrowed for a moment. "You're not Johnny Callaghan. You look like him, but you don't act like him, and you certainly don't sound like him."

"Sound? What? My voice?"

She shook her head, one curl of hair loosening in the gesture. "No, your vocabulary. You've used words no one else in town knows but me. Some of them, even *I* don't know the meaning of! Whoever you are, you're not

Johnny." She unwrapped the ring and examined the engraving on the inner band. "I mean, *our* Johnny. I guess you're . . ." She stared up at him. "John B. Callaghan the Fifth." She slipped the ring on her thumb.

"Actually it's John Barrett Callan, the Fifth."

Emma glanced up from her perusal. "You mean you're not Johnny's—" She extended her fingers to tick off the generations. "—great-great-grandson?"

"Yeah, I am, but somewhere down the line one of the 'greats' changed it from Callaghan to Callan. A little less ethnic, I guess. John is my first name, but everybody calls me Barrett."

"Oh. Barrett." She sounded as if she were test-driving the name and found it satisfactory. After a moment of intense study, Emma caught him in a steely stare. "Barrett C-Callan, I have a question about the future."

He tried to smile. "Only one?"

"Of course not." A quick look of irritation crossed her face. "I have a billion questions about the things to come. But first things first."

"What?" His mind raced ahead. The next president? Next war? If this was any other woman but Emma Nolan, he'd expect a question about the fashions of the next century.

"Sherlock Holmes!" An unexpected beauty

shone through her excitement as she became suddenly animated. "How many stories will . . . er . . . did Dr. Doyle write? You mentioned something about Sherlock dying but being brought back to life. When does this happen? How long will I have to wait for him to pick up the stories again?"

Barrett's mind went blank. Already he had blurted out just about all he'd remembered in the discussion about Holmes earlier. He certainly didn't recall the dates of publication, much less the titles of Sir Arthur Conan Doyle's entire works.

"Well?" She stood, balancing her hands on her hips.

He shrugged. "I don't remember." At her impatient expression, he added. "Why can't you ask me about who the next president will be? Or who won the space race? Or World War Two?"

The color and exuberance drained from her face. "S-space? War?" She reached out for the bedside table with an unsteady hand. "I . . . I don't feel so good."

Barrett recognized the signs; she was going to faint if he didn't do something. "Emma, sit down and put your head between your knees. You'll feel better. I promise." He helped her to bend over.

She complied, her words muffled by her skirts.

"What did you say?" He reached over intending to pat her back, but withdrew his hand, unsure how to comfort her.

Her only answer was a groan.

"Emma?"

When she sat up, her ashen face had regained a little color. "I feel so . . . so foolish."

"Why? Because you reacted like anybody else to news which is pretty spectacular? And pretty unbelievable, too?"

She gave him a wan smile. "But to get all giddy and to almost . . ."

"Swoon? Faint? Keel over? Black out?"

Emma swatted at his arm. "You don't have to rub it in, Joh . . . uh . . . Barrett." Her smile grew a little. "Please, don't tell anyone I reacted like this."

It was his turn to grin. "You think I'm going to run around telling everybody I meet that when I told you I was a time-traveler from the late twentieth century, you had the audacity to almost faint? They'll lock me up in the nearest loony bin and throw away the key, then they'll make you the mayor of Margin."

"Mayor? Me?" Her laughter returned in full force. "You must come from a wonderful future where women can be mayors. And doctors."

"Where I come from . . ." He paused. "No, it's not as much *where* but *when* I come from, women can be pretty much anything they want to be. There are still some inequities left, but things are changing."

Emma became a rapt audience, leading him with astute questions about life in the twentieth century. He admitted to himself later that he'd painted a rather rosy view of his world, but in retrospect, he realized he was indeed lucky to live in a time of so many technical advances. Emma seemed to agree.

". . . so when Johnny offered to change places with you, you accepted? Just like that? Leaving behind your motor cars and your instant ovens? And your tele-vision?" The light bulb of cognition formed in her eyes. "Television. TV! That's what you were muttering about. It *was* a thing, not a person. What about a 'remote'? Does it have something to do with tele-vision, too?"

Their animated conversation continued with such energy that Barrett didn't hear his landlady's usual thundering hoofbeats until the door swung open. Miss Penny stepped in, balancing a tray in her hands. Her face matched the red checked cloth covering the plate.

"Sheriff? Emma! What's all this laughing about? Jimmie told me you'd come back early because you was feelin' puny." Although she failed to say aloud that Barrett looked anything but "puny" in person, her eyes spelled out her disappointment. She eyed Emma's flushed face and gave Barrett a once-over, settling on the flesh exposed by his open shirt.

Emma recovered first.

"Oh, Penny! You are the dearest, most thoughtful person. I was trying to keep—" She stuttered over his name. ". . . J-Johnny from overdoing it, and you have the perfect solution. A sickroom dinner. Here, I'll move." Emma stood up and offered Penny the chair.

Barrett felt his blood pressure take a sharp jump into the stratosphere.

Emma gave him a sickeningly sweet smile, laced with "I've Got A Secret" highlights in her eyes. "I have papers to grade tonight. I'll drop by *later* and check on how you're doing, Sheriff. Enjoy your dinner." She paused just long enough to slip him a wink behind Penny's back, then left.

Penny flipped back the cloth to reveal a steaming bowl of stew. She scooped up a spoonful of meat chunks and shoved it in the vicinity of Barrett's mouth. "You don't look like you're feelin' so bad, Sheriff."

Barrett took the spoon from her pudgy fingers. "It's the medicine, Miss Penny. Just the medicine."

After supper, Emma bowed to the pressure to grade Ford's paper first. Usually test questions generated answers from the near-ignorant to the truly inspired and every degree in between. Ford had the native intelligence to rise to the top of the class, but lacked the ambition to reach his potential. Unfortunately, this time his answers employed more creative license than accuracy. Upon learning his score, Emma banned her brother to his room to study, then started on the rest of the papers.

Although she tried desperately to concentrate on grading, her mind wandered back to Johnny—she corrected herself—Barrett Callan. Unfortunately Sherlock Holmes had offered no sage advice to cover the situation when she eliminated both the implausible and the impossible. All she had left was the gut feeling that the man calling himself Barrett Callan truly was from another time, another place. It was the only explanation which made sense.

Sense?

Emma laughed. Nothing Barrett had said made much sense, but in a way it did have a ring of truth to it. A class ring from 1985, to be exact. She smiled at her own jest and tried to turn her attention back to her work. After finishing the last paper, she dutifully recorded the scores, then refreshed herself with a cup of coffee.

As she drank, she mulled over thoughts of the future. What did people do in the future? What did they eat? What forms of transportation had evolved in the ensuing hundred years?

Emma found a clean page in her journal and began to jot down questions to ask Barrett.

Food.
Transportation.
Schools.
World events.

The clouds which had muffled the moon parted and a silver ray highlighted Emma's paper. After a moment she got up, carried her cup to the window, glanced out, and made an automatic wish on the first star.

Wish I may, wish I might . . .

Did people in the late twentieth century still do silly things like make wishes on stars? Barrett had mentioned a race in space, supporting another of Mr. Verne's stories about men traveling to the moon in a spaceship.

Space travel, time travel . . . where did it end?

Emma looked at the moon.

So much to learn . . .

"You what?!"

Barrett continued to make minute adjustments to the blotter on Johnny's desk. "I told Emma who I was and where I was from," he repeated. After stealing a quick glance at Harvey, Barrett turned his attention back to the blotter.

His companion began to pace the room. "Of all the lame-brained, stupid, inherently asinine things to do!" He paused in mid-step. "You do realize how much STC damage you could've caused by telling her about the future?"

Barrett tried to look only mildly confused. "STP what?"

"STC damage. You know, Space-Time Continuum?" Harvey stared at Barrett for a moment, then shook his head. "I guess it's back to school time. Okay, you know how time is the fourth dimension, right?"

It was an opening Barrett couldn't resist. "I remember the Fifth Dimension. Great group, good harmonies."

"Listen you idiot, do you want to learn how you may have ripped up the universe, or do you want to play Trivial Compute?"

"Pursuit."

"What?"

"It's called Trivial Pursuit."

Harvey slapped his forehead with his palm. "I'm being serious here! Pay attention." He pointed at a pencil on the desk. "The first three dimensions tell us what an object is in size and shape, and the fourth dimension tells us when it is."

Barrett stumbled over the word. "W-when . . ."

"Look." Harvey reached into his vest and pulled out his watch. From its darkened face, he extracted a very cheap, but very modern, ballpoint pen. "Keep your eye on this." He placed the pen so it touched the pencil, then stalked across the room into the farthermost jail cell. He still cradled the watch in his hand. "I'm . . . what?" he called out. "Maybe twenty feet away from the desk?"

Barrett mentally measured the distance and nodded.

"Now keep watching the pen," Harvey ordered.

Barrett stared at the pen.

Nothing happened.

He waited for another full minute before shifting his glance to his companion. "I don't—"

"Just shut up and watch."

Another minute went by before Barrett noticed anything. As he stared at the pen, its edges stared to blur. He squinted and rubbed one eye, wondering why his eyesight would start to bother him now.

"It's not your eyes." Harvey sounded smug but Barrett was too interested in the unfolding spectacle to shift his attention.

The tip of the pen disappeared first. Then the body of the pen turned glittery and slowly dissolved to nothing. One moment it was there, the next . . . gone.

Barrett stared at the emptiness. He'd seen

a similar dissolution before. The irritating sense of déjà vu perched on the front edge of his mind until he suddenly realized where he'd seen the process before.

"I get it. You transported it, right? You know, like . . . 'Beam me up, Scotty!'?"

Harvey stalked back across the room to the desk. "Jeez, it was *only* a television show . . ." He released a theatrical sigh. "No, I didn't 'transport' it. When I go back in time, I have to escape the influence of the fourth dimension which wants to keep me in my proper place in time. The portal watch acts as a time stabilizer. Without it, my molecules couldn't keep from flying apart because they lack the element of time to hold them in the right place."

He pointed to the desk. "Once the pen from the future was out of the sphere of the portal watch, its three dimensions reacted with the existing fourth dimension here, and they were incompatible. Do you understand what that means?"

Barrett contemplated the empty space. "It means you have to keep the watch with you at all times. Or you're likely to . . . fly off the handle!"

"I can't believe someone's letting you fly around in time without any understanding of temporal theory and application." Harvey tightened his fist and took a swipe at the desk. "You're breaking every law of physics and nature, just being here. But you're just not only a danger to yourself." He pointed to the pencil on the desk. "Pick that up."

When Barrett reached for the pencil, it sagged in his fingers like a bad joke from a novelty shop. Draped across the palm of his hand, the rubberized wood shaft shimmered, then disintegrated into splinters, and the lead liquefied into a dark puddle.

Harvey spoke in an ominous Darth Vader voice. "Temporal instability not only affects the object itself, but its nearby surroundings as well. You shouldn't be able to exist in this century without a portal watch or something similar. You are an anomaly."

Barrett toyed with the pencil remains, watching the splinters turn into a powder. "I've been called worse . . ."

"You, my friend, are either the world's luckiest fool . . ." Harvey dropped into a chair by the desk without continuing his statement.

"Or what?"

Harvey eyed Barrett. "Or the world's most dangerous man."

Eight

Barrett searched through the desk drawer, looking for another pencil to replace the one destroyed by the lesson in time theory. When he found a broken stub and a jackknife, he had to smile.

John Barrett Callan, the Third, a.k.a. Grandpa John, had tried to educate his only grandson on the niceties of whittling. They'd sit on the porch, creating a pile of wood shavings which always seemed more interesting than the carvings themselves. Barrett usually gave up early in the creation process, being content to fiddle with the wonderfully long curls of wood which Grandpa John produced with the smooth even strokes of his knife.

Barrett's first adult attempt with a sharp blade resulted in a lopsided pencil point and two near-misses with his thumb. Despite the near-bloodletting, the hook of nostalgia had been set. Damn the waiting paperwork! Barrett found a suitable stick in the firewood bin and settled back in his chair for some serious whittling.

As he created his own pile of curled wood shavings, his mind drifted back to last night's animated conversation with Emma. When he told Harvey how readily she'd absorbed the information about the future, the time-traveler nearly had a seizure right there in the office. Harvey spent the better part of the next two hours explaining to Barrett how time rifts were created through premature information exchange. Or as the man succinctly put it, "Shooting holes in the fabric of time by shooting off your mouth."

When Emma burst into the office without even knocking, the sharp knife bit into Barrett's forefinger.

"Damn it, Emma. Can't you give a guy some warning?" He sucked at the wound, then pinched it, hoping to stem the bleeding.

She scanned the room quickly. "Anyone here?" She continued without even waiting for an answer. "I have so many questions to ask about the way things are going to be." She stripped off her hat and threw it in the general direction of the desk. "First, what kind of changes have happened in the medical field?" The grey cloak landed across the back of the chair with reasonable accuracy. "What can you do in the future that we can't now . . . medically speaking?"

Now, for the first time...

You can find
Janelle Taylor, Shannon
Drake, Rosanne Bittner,
Sylvie Sommerfield,
Penelope Neri, Phoebe
Conn, Bobbi Smith,
and the rest of
today's most popular,
bestselling authors

*...All in one
brand-new club!*

Introducing
KENSINGTON CHOICE,
the new Zebra/Pinnacle service
that delivers the best
new historical romances
direct to your home,
at a significant discount
off the publisher's prices.

As your
introduction,
we invite you
to accept
4 FREE BOOKS
worth up to $23.96
details inside...

We've got your authors!

If you seek out the latest historical romances by today's bestselling authors, our new reader's service, KENSINGTON CHOICE, is the club for you.

KENSINGTON CHOICE is the only club where you can find authors like Janelle Taylor, Shannon Drake, Rosanne Bittner, Sylvie Sommerfield, Penelope Neri and Phoebe Conn all in one place...

...and the only service that will deliver their romances direct to your home as soon as they are published—even before they reach the bookstores.

KENSINGTON CHOICE is also the only service that will give you a substantial guaranteed discount off the publisher's prices on every one of those romances.

That's right: Every month, the Editors at Zebra and Pinnacle select four of the newest novels by our bestselling authors and rush them straight to you, usually *before they reach the bookstores*. The publisher's prices for these romances range from $4.99 to $5.99—but they are always yours for the guaranteed low price of just *$4.20!*

That means you'll always save over 20% off the publisher's prices on every shipment you get from KENSINGTON CHOICE!

All books are sent on a 10-day free examination basis, and there is no minimum number of books to buy. (A postage and handling charge of $1.50 is added to each shipment.)

As your introduction to the convenience and value of this new service, we invite you to accept

4 BOOKS FREE

The 4 books, worth up to $23.96, are our welcoming gift. You pay only $1 to help cover postage and handling.

To start your subscription to KENSINGTON CHOICE and receive your introductory package of 4 FREE romances, detach and mail the card at right *today.*

We have 4 FREE BOOKS for you
as your introduction to
KENSINGTON CHOICE
To get your FREE BOOKS, worth
up to $23.96, mail the card below.

FREE BOOK CERTIFICATE

As my introduction to your new KENSINGTON CHOICE reader's service, please send me 4 FREE historical romances (worth up to $23.96), billing me just $1 to help cover postage and handling. As a KENSINGTON CHOICE subscriber, I will then receive 4 brand-new romances to preview each month for 10 days FREE. I can return any books I decide not to keep and owe nothing. The publisher's prices for the KENSINGTON CHOICE romances range from $4.99 to $5.99, but as a subscriber I will be entitled to get them for just $4.20 per book or $16.80 for all four titles. There is no minimum number of books to buy, and I can cancel my subscription at any time. A $1.50 postage and handling charge is added to each shipment.

Name _____

Address _____ Apt. _____

City _____ State _____ Zip _____

Telephone ( ) _____

Signature _____

(If under 18, parent or guardian must sign)

Subscription subject to acceptance. Terms and prices subject to change.

KC0995

Barrett stared at her. What shouldn't he tell her about? Blood transfusions? Immunizations against polio and a host of other diseases? Organ transplants? AIDS?

Harvey's words began to echo in Barrett's mind. For a sudden moment, every movie and television show he'd ever seen about time travel flashed through his head. How much future was he willing to change? How much was too much? Would one small pebble of information offered now cause a technological *tsunami* in the future?

"Well?" She dropped into the chair and leaned expectantly on his desk.

"Emma, I . . . I can't."

"Why?" She shifted closer, smelling of chalk and flowers.

"Because . . ." He hesitated for a moment. "Because I might change too much of the future."

"Too much? How in the heavens could you do that?"

"Suppose you knew the outcome of the next presidential election. Would you bother voting if you already knew who won?"

"But you were willing to tell me so much yesterday. What's changed between yesterday and to—hey, wait a minute." Her initial look of confusion transformed to one of gleaming excitement. "Women get the right to vote, don't they?" She began to grin. "When? How?"

Barrett swallowed hard. *One object lesson bites the dust.* Even in his efforts not to reveal anything, he'd divulged plenty. He pushed back away from her. "Please, Emma . . . don't ask me these things. I was never a good student and what I do remember is probably wrong."

She slammed her hand against the desk in obvious irritation. "You just can't waltz in here, announce you're from the future, and expect me not to be curious about what lies ahead."

"Emma, if it were just curiosity, it'd be all right. But it's more than that. I'm not a doctor; I can't tell you exactly how the medical procedures are performed in my time."

"I don't have to have exact details." She folded her hands in sudden contrition. "Just a general idea."

"I can't . . ."

"So why did you come here? To laugh at our backward ways?" She made a face. "I assume we appear terribly primitive to a man who can travel through time." Storm clouds deepened her blue gaze, reminding him of the first time they'd met, All that steel and armor protecting a compassionate heart beneath.

"Emma, that's not it." Barrett ran his hand through his hair. "I didn't come here in a time machine; it was more like a stroke of dumb luck."

She crossed her arms, wearing her suspicion and a stroke of chalk dust on her sleeve. "Dumb luck?"

"I'm no mad scientist, no genius with a fistful of degrees. I'm not here to laugh at you, or study the past, or anything except to clear my name."

"Your name? How?"

He shifted in his chair, trying to find a comfortable position. "It's a long story."

Emma raised a mocking eyebrow. "I have plenty of *time* . . ."

An hour later, Barrett and Emma had a survey map spread across the desk. He pointed to a familiar spot. "The mine entrance is here?"

Emma reached down and shifted his finger a half inch over to the left. "No, here."

Barrett made a rapid calculation, tracing his way along the map. "Seventy-eight from the outcropping entrance, the shaft branches. The left branch takes off at a thirty degree angle and the right branch travels another hundred and five before it splits with a second branch taking off to the right at a sixty-two degree angle." He found the pencil and sketched the shaft locations on the paper, stabbing the right branch so hard that the pencil point broke. "The copper starts here. The vein follows the fissure for fifty-eight feet, then angles off to the right. That's where we got into problems."

Emma stared at the hand-drawn shafts. "What do you mean?"

"Look." He pointed to the map. "Here's the outcropping and here's the place where the copper vein angles away. The distance is . . ." He jockeyed some numbers in the margin of the map. " . . . roughly two hundred and thirty feet, lateral."

"And?"

"It puts the end of the shaft roughly here. Under Main Street."

She stared at the map, her expression narrowing to one of intense concentration. Her words started hesitantly. "And the common town properties are held jointly by the founding families of Margin."

"Which means . . ." he supplied.

"Which means in order to mine the land, you'd have to negotiate the mineral rights with . . . virtually everybody in town."

He nodded. "Which is exactly what Thornwald did. Everybody signed their property over to him right before the silver industry collapsed. At least that's the version I was told all my life. Johnny told me Thornwald actually blew up the mine in order to trick the people into believing it was played out. Of course, Johnny didn't know that when he formed a partnership with Thornwald. Together they created the Continental

Silver and Copper Consortium, but Thornwald and his heirs always kept the property rights, which eventually got tangled up in red tape and family legalities. When my company, Callan Industries, was all that was left of the original partnership, we didn't have the land rights and it's slowly choked the life out of our business."

"So you want to grab the land before Thornwald does?"

He shrugged. "In essence."

She glanced up from the map, cocking her head at him. "What makes *you* any better than *him*?"

"Huh?"

Emma leaned back in the chair. "People thought they were selling worthless land to Thornwald, correct?" She didn't wait for an answer. "So I suspect he didn't have to pay much to get the mining rights."

Barrett nodded. "That's probably true."

"So all you're going to do is get a jump on him by cheating the people out of their property first."

"Well, not cheating . . ."

She crossed her arms with great precision. "It's still cheating, not telling them there's a good reason to hold on to the land. And I won't help you."

"But Emma—"

"But nothing! I won't help you swindle the

townspeople of Margin. I can't believe any kinsman of Johnny Cal—"

He thundered the words in his best boardroom voice. "Emma, shut up."

She glared at him, undaunted by the tone which in his own time had cowed a host of irate vice presidents, stopped meter maids in their tracks, and won the best tables from uncooperative maître d's.

"—laghan would stoop to defraud the people out of their just due."

For a moment they were at a stalemate, both glowering at each other, then Barrett decided to make the first defensive move. "Emma, I'm not going to trick the people into selling me the land."

She raised one eyebrow.

"I'm going to suggest they unite against Thornwald and form their own company—"

"With you as the president . . ." she supplied.

"Someone has to protect their interests. It might as well be me. Anyway, the way Johnny figured it, when I finish setting up the changes in the past, I'll leave and return to a new future. Everything in my world will be different. How different, I won't know until I get back."

"Well . . ." She appeared unconvinced.

"Look, you might not trust me, Emma, but you do trust Johnny, don't you?"

She nodded, albeit reluctantly.

Barrett continued. "So my motives aren't in question at all because no matter what I do, Johnny's the one who ends up in control. Right?"

Emma took a few seconds to mull over his words before releasing a deep breath. "You're a lot like Johnny." She rewarded Barrett with a guarded smile. "Logical to a fault."

He returned her grin. "I can think of worse faults to have."

"Me, too." She turned her attention back to the map. "There's one thing which bothers me."

"What?"

"Why does Thornwald want the mining rights so badly? How could he know about a copper vein which according to you hasn't been discovered yet?"

Barrett stared at her. "I never thought about that."

She pointed out the window. "Well, you better start thinking about it. Here he comes, now."

A harried moment later, Thornwald entered the office waving a piece of paper in his hand. "Sheriff, I just received a telegram. The bank robbers have been caught in Colorado Springs."

"That was fast."

"The swift and mighty arm of justice prevails." The man wore a smug look.

Barrett glanced at the telegram. "I find it odd that you received notice of their capture before I did. Friends in high places?"

Thornwald flushed for a brief moment, but recovered with admirable speed. "What's the use of having friends if they aren't in a position to help?" He dropped the paper on Barrett's desk. "But our security precautions weren't in vain. We'll be prepared should another situation like that crop up. 'Though I must say I'm delighted to discover another literate soul in this . . ." Thornwald made a careless encompassing gesture with his manicured hand. ". . . this backwater, this hellhole."

"I'm surprised this town holds any appeal for a man of your evident erudition and obvious education." Barrett indicated the vacant chair at the end of the desk.

Thornwald slipped on an oily smile and pulled out a handkerchief to dust the seat before sitting. He leaned his silver-knobbed cane against the edge of the desk. "I, sir, am an entrepreneur." He pronounced the word with deliberate pride.

Barrett stretched back in his chair. "And here I thought you were merely a bank manager."

"Ah . . . a common misconception. They are not what I'd call mutually exclusive terms."

Barrett thought about the savings and loan

scandals in his own time. *Wanna bet?* "I suppose a banker has to be as fiscally alert as any other enterprising business owner with an eye for profit."

"Exactly." The smarmy smile grew wider. "And like a man of enterprise, I'm always on the lookout for opportunities to . . ." His voice trailed off as he scanned the room. His gaze settled on the blanket-covered figure stretched out on the jail cell cot.

Barrett shook his head. "Don't mind our friend over there. He's in no shape to listen in on our private conversation." He paused. "I *do* suspect you'd like to make our discussion here a private matter."

"Indeed I would." Thornwald leaned closer and lowered his voice. "You mentioned earlier about my friends in high places. Some of those friends have told me about some disturbing legislation which will adversely affect the price of silver. If it passes, it'll devastate this entire area."

"Really?"

"Indeed, sir. The town of Margin will cease to exist almost overnight when the mines fail. The townspeople will lose their livelihood, their money, and their properties unless we do something to help them."

"Help them? How?" Barrett studied the man's face, unable to reconcile the words of sympathy with the lack of human compassion in his cold eyes.

"I know many wealthy people who do not have the . . . contacts I do in Washington. They aren't aware of the impending legislation. If they are presented with an opportunity to purchase a successful silver mining operation, I'm sure they'd jump at the chance to speculate."

"So what does this have to do with the townspeople? I'd think you'd want to approach the mine owners with the offer."

"Oh I have," Thornwald answered too quickly. "Negotiations have started already. But there is a matter about additional land which involves the town's joint cooperation." The banker scanned the room. "Have you a map of the area?"

Barrett almost said yes, then belatedly remembered the neat sketches which outlined the entire mine shaft locations, including the hitherto undiscovered copper vein. "Uh, no," he lied. He reached into his drawer and pulled out a clean sheet of paper. "Would this help?"

The banker waved aside Barrett's offer of a pencil and removed a fountain pen from his inner coat pocket. With a few inky scratches, Thornwald had drawn a rough but basically accurate draft of the mine. "I know my buyers will be interested in more than just the existing properties. I believe they'll want to purchase additional land with an eye toward expansion." The man stabbed the paper, leaving a large blot of ink to mark the center of town. "It's logical to plan growth in this direction, traveling along an existing shaft."

"And just how do I fit into the picture?"

Thornwald capped his pen. "Sheriff . . . I haven't been here long enough to understand the internal politics of the town, but I have learned who these people admire and look up to: you. If you assure them this is a legitimate offer, backed by honest money, they'll believe you."

Barrett riveted his undivided attention to the map, hoping to shake the man's confidence with the hesitation. After a suitably long time, Barrett glanced up. "But *I* have to believe *you*, first." He added a smile. "And I don't."

"But Sheriff, I assure you this is a legitimate offer," the man sputtered. "Without me, the people in this town stand to lose everything."

"Mr. Thornwald, I believe the people in this town stand to lose even more if they fall for your cockamamie scheme."

"But . . ." The man rose, his knuckles whitening as he grabbed his cane. "You don't realize the chance you're throwing away. I'll . . . I'll cut you in for a percentage. How about ten percent . . . as a finder's fee?"

"I can't find what hasn't been lost, Alphonse." Barrett smiled at the man's shocked expression. "Yes, I do know a great deal about you. More than you'd probably want to know." *Died at age seventy-three in the arms of your third wife the stripper, who promptly tied up your grown children's inheritance in litigation.* Barrett added a prayer of thanks to his Grandpa John who used their whittling time to regale his grandson with stories of their family's business origins.

Thornwald blustered out of the room, leaving behind him a cloud of thinly veiled threats and useless predictions of financial ruin for the town. After the echoes had died away, a muffled voice called out from the jail cell.

"Is he gone?"

Barrett stood at the window, watching the man stomp back toward the bank. "The coast is clear."

Emma threw back the blanket and fanned her face. "I don't know which was worse: the smell, the heat, or listening to that . . . that odorous man. How dare he think he can go in cahoots with you to bilk the townspeople out of their land over some vague rumors about silver legislation." She stood up, trying to brush her skirt back into proper repair.

"Problem is . . ." Barrett paused to scratch his head. "He's right. There's legislation brewing in Washington which will undermine the silver industry early next year."

"Then why does he want the land? Surely any investors with enough money to purchase the mining operation will likely have the same type of informational contacts in the government." She plucked at some stray curls which trickled down her neck. "If he knows the price of silver will drop, why does he still want the mine?"

For a brief moment, Barrett wondered what she'd look like with her hair down, literally and figuratively. He shook himself back into the conversation. "Uh . . . good question. There has to be more at stake here. But what?"

"If you don't know . . . who does?"

"Only Thornwald. But I don't think he'll be willing to tell us the truth. Not when the almighty buck is on the line." Barrett paused to glance at the telegram detailing the capture of the bank robbers. "It's getting to the point where you need a score card to tell the bad guys from the good guys."

Nine

Persuasion, Barrett decided, came in all forms: flattery, logic, social conscience, and sometimes, out-and-out lies. When it came to persuading people to think in one unified direction, Barrett employed whichever method he thought applicable, but he found himself increasingly bothered by the last option.

Somehow, he couldn't quite bring it upon himself to lie to the people of Margin. Not even for their own good. Of course, when it came to conversing with Silas Brainard, the truth took on an interesting twist.

"Well, Silas, I can't tell you what to do, only your conscience can do that. But if I were you . . ." Barrett reached down and ruffled the red hair of the drippy-nosed child smearing peppermint on his pant leg. "I'd sure want to leave something more than cold cash as a legacy to my children. Miss Emma says this little guy's older brother holds great promise in the schoolroom. I'm sure he's going to make a fine grocer just like his Pa."

Silas Brainard's posture puffed with the conceit of paternal pride, and he gave his progeny a loving glance. "I always did say Junior inherited more than just his good looks from me. He's got my head for figures, too."

Barrett neglected to relate Emma's entire assessment of Junior Brainard's abilities, in which she cited his brute strength as his best attribute when it came to moving things in his father's storeroom. The only "figure" which impressed the boy was that of a comely thirteen-year-old who delighted in sending him teasing winks across the school-room every day.

Another redheaded moppet bounced into the room, blithely stole her brother's candy stick, and beat a hasty retreat. The boy re-vealed an impressive vocabulary and a re-markable set of lungs as he tore off after his sister, screaming of retributions which made even Barrett blush.

The grocer offered a "kids will be kids" shrug and continued. "So you believe I shouldn't sell out to Thornwald?"

"Absolutely not. There's something fishy about this man and his offer." Barrett leaned forward in obvious conspiracy. "His offer is just too good to be true. I don't *trust* him."

Trust.

Barrett had quickly learned the value of the word as well as the merit of Johnny Callaghan's sterling reputation when it came to swaying people. It was the sort of status politicians could only dream of. One word, one mere whispered suggestion of caution from Sheriff Johnny B. Callaghan, Upstanding Citizen Extraordinaire, and the people of Margin instantly agreed not to sell.

It was simple.

Too damn simple in Barrett's opinion, but he wasn't one to closely examine a gift horse's dental work. By the next afternoon, he had a verbal arrangement with every common landholder in town, all of them agreeing to retain possession of their joint lands. Barrett didn't want to push them into any formal organization, figuring it would be a fallback offensive position to use only if his defensive strategies failed.

Once he finished with Silas, Barrett returned to his office and checked the grocer's name off the list. Only one person remained. It gave Barrett chills to consider what wiles he would need to employ in order to persuade the last of Margin's founding fathers. Or mothers, as the case might be.

Barrett girded his loins and headed across the street.

As soon as Penny saw him, a grin split her

wide face. "Sheriff! You'll be pleased to know I fixed your favorite foods tonight."

He allowed himself to be hauled across the room to what was considered Penny's "By Invitation Only" table. She looked as if she'd like to tuck the napkin under his chin herself, but he forestalled her by grabbing it first. But as she served him the heaping platter of chicken and plopped a pint of mashed potatoes on his plate, he uttered the very words which Emma had assured him would win the landlady's undying loyalty and gratitude.

"Will you join me for dinner, Miss Penny?"

Her shock turned to gleaming pleasure as she dropped into the chair next to him. "This is so . . . so sudden, Sheriff." Her eyelashes fluttered at warp speed, and her pudgy fingers snaked across the gingham tablecloth toward his hand.

Barrett decided it was high time to enjoy his supper and that he would need both hands to perform such a daunting task. He didn't have to worry about conversation, since he was unable to get a word in edgewise. She prattled about the weather, the food, and her latest reading material, pausing only to devour enough food to feed the Green Bay Packers.

During training season.

After his fourth piece of chicken, Barrett

discovered his stomach would tolerate no more stalling tactics. He pushed back from the table and gave his hostess a pained but calculated smile. "I don't think I've ever met anybody who can cook like you do. You're a real artist in the kitchen, Miss Penny."

The blush started above her third chin and disappeared into the Grand Canyon of cleavages. "An artist? Oh, Sheriff, the things you say . . ." Her hand wormed its way toward his again.

Distraction! "Uh . . . how about some of that wonderful-looking apple pie over there? It smells heavenly."

She hesitated for a moment, then smiled. "I'll serve you myself."

As she lumbered over to the sideboard, Barrett closed his eyes and sent up a short-wave prayer of help; would someone, even some*thing,* save him from his amorous land-lady?

Penny returned with a quarter of the entire pie crowded onto one small plate. "I only cut you one slice, but there's more if you'd like."

When he eyed the slab of pastry, his entire body screamed in protest. But duty demanded that Barrett turn to her and give her the best smile he could muster for the occasion. "L-looks delicious." He grabbed the fork and held it over the pie. "Hmmm boy, de-li-cious."

He waited until he'd reached his absolute

apple saturation point before broaching the subject of the banker's offers. In the middle of his "trust" speech, Penny waved her hand in protest.

"You don't have to say another word. That greasy feller already came in here, talking money. He sat himself down at this very table without as much as a 'how-de-do' and tried to convince me to sell. I put a piece of pie down in front of him, and he had the audacity to turn it down. Said he couldn't eat rich food 'cause of his digestion. Digestion!" She snorted, gesturing with her knife. "I'll tell you what! Any thin-as-a-rail man who looks at a piece of Penny Butterworth's pie and tells you he ain't hungry is either sick, lying, or a fool."

Barrett bulldozed another load of apples to his mouth out of necessity. "So which is he?"

Her gaze narrowed. "He ain't sick, so he's either a foolish liar or a lying fool. No matter which, I wouldn't give him the time of day, much less sell him the rights to this land. Like you said . . . I'm an artist, and an artist has to have some place where she can keep creating." Her expression softened as Barrett ate the last bite of her monument to Life, Liberty and the American Way. "I like a man who can enjoy a good apple pie."

Panic began to rise in his stomach, jostling the pie along the way. "Well, I—"

"Sheriff?" Ford Nolan appeared at the table.

Barrett almost wanted to kiss the little guy. "What's wrong, Ford?"

Before the child could say anything, Penny barked out his name. "Young man . . ." She pointed to his hat.

Ford ripped the offensive headgear from his head. "Sorry, Miss Penny. Uh, Sheriff, the deputy needs you back at the office at once."

Before Barrett could react, Penny swooped over, snatched up the napkin from his lap, and proceeded to wipe the crumbs from his mouth. "You better go on, Sheriff. At least I know you've got a good home-cooked meal in your belly to keep you warm tonight." Her expression said *she'd* rather be the one to keep him warm.

Barrett almost ran out of the restaurant, dragging Ford with him. As soon as they were out of range of Penny's curious stare, Barrett reached into his pocket and pulled out a nickel. "Here." He flipped it to Ford. "You really deserve it this time, kid."

"What about me? I'm the one who sent him."

Barrett pivoted, grinned, and reached into his pocket again. He pressed the second nickel into Emma's outstretched hand. "Next time, send Ford before dessert. In my time, we have the Geneva Convention, which protects prisoners of war from cruel and unusual punishment."

Emma grinned. "And all this while, I thought you were a prisoner of love. Did it work? Did Penny agree?"

Barrett led the way to his office. "I've got to give her credit. She'd already pegged Thornwald as a louse. For all her faults, she knows a crook when she sees—Hey!" Barrett reacted fast enough to pull Emma out of the way of a body which was hurtling out of the doors of the Crystal Plume. The man landed in the street, sending up a puff of dust to herald his ungainly arrival.

"And stay out!" Earl the bartender stood on the threshold of the swinging doors, holding a truncheon in one hand. He nodded affably to Barrett. "Sheriff. Miss Emma."

Barrett found himself with a protective arm around Emma's waist, and although he loathed letting her go, a sense of duty—albeit Johnny's duty—called. He moved her behind him and turned to the bartender. "Having a problem, Earl?"

Earl shook his head while tapping the bat in the palm of his hand. "Not really. I just told this . . . this *interluder* he's not welcome here."

Barrett winced inside. *That's "interloper,"*
Earl.

The figure sprawled in the street began to stir. When the man turned his head to the halo of the gas street light, Barrett recognized the miner who had shot him. Before he could say anything, Earl shook a fist at the man.

"McConnell, I thought you were bright enough to stay out of the saloon for a while."

"Ah jest wanted a drink," McConnell mumbled, brushing the loose dirt from his filthy shirt.

Emma stepped out from behind Barrett. "Mr. McConnell, there's nothing wrong with a man lifting a glass after a hard's day work. But I'm afraid you've abused that privilege."

The man squinted at her, evidently unable to focus well. "You the pretty thang from the saloon?"

As the man lumbered to his feet, Barrett stepped forward again, shielding Emma from what he considered an unnecessary danger. "McConnell, you stay away from the lady."

"Not gonna hurt her." He wiped a streak of mud from his face. "Gonna 'pologize." He looked up with bloodshot eyes. "I'm sorry I scared you, ma'am." His face reddened and he turned toward Barrett. "And I'm sorry I shot ya, Sheriff. Never shot a man before. Never want to again."

Before Barrett could say anything, Emma

pushed past him again. "I consider it a fair apology, Mr. McConnell. And I accept. But . . ." She turned back and gave Barrett a hooded glance. "I'm not so sure just an apology will do in the sheriff's case. Sheriff . . ." Her eyes widened, transmitting a thousand messages to Barrett, the most important being, "Follow my lead."

She continued. "Sheriff, you were mentioning to me something about having Mr. McConnell pay restitution to the town for disrupting your civic responsibilities."

McConnell stared at her. "Huh?"

Emma nodded. "It's only fair that you perform some municipally oriented duty to repay for the inconvenience you've caused the townspeople."

McConnell continued to squint. "Lady, I can't understand a word you're sayin'."

Earl leaned on his bat. "She means they're gonna make you work 'cause you shot the sheriff."

"Oh . . ." McConnell shrugged. "Well, I 'spose it's only fair." He gave them a tentative, toothless smile. "So whatcha want me to do, Sheriff?"

Barrett hesitated.

Emma jumped in. "Garbage, Mr. McConnell."

He gaped at her. "Pardon?"

"Garbage. Refuse. Trash. It builds in the

streets and in the alleys. It's a health hazard to the people of Margin."

McConnell lost his glazed stare, shifting to one of sheer amazement. "You want me to pick up trash?"

Barrett smiled. "Not just 'pick up trash,' McConnell. You'll be the town's only refuse collector, an honorable and necessary profession." He almost blurted out "time-honored" but stopped himself in time.

"Just think about the possibilities . . ." Barrett gestured toward the street. "Your colleagues rise before the sun, work in a dirty hole in the ground, then stumble home after dark. They are no more than a cog in the impersonal mining machinery of life. But, as a Refuse Collector, you become the most important man in town, hauling away the trash to leave Margin neater and safer." After taking a deep breath, Barrett put his arm around the man's odorous shoulders. "Just imagine . . . you start with the trash from the east side of the street on Mondays and Thursdays. Everybody has to get up early just to meet *your* schedule. Then it's the west side of the street on Tuesdays and Fridays. And want to know the best part?"

McConnell gaped, showing how deep the hook, line, and sinker had penetrated. "What, Sheriff?" he asked in a hushed voice.

Barrett leaned closer, giving the man a

conspiratorial wink. "You get to keep anything good you find."

The man's face lit up. "Really? Anything? Oh, Sheriff . . ." He began to pump Barrett's hand with unbridled enthusiasm. "How can I thank you? I promise I won't let you down. I'll be the best Ref . . . ref . . ."

"Refuse Collector," Emma supplied.

McConnell stumbled over the words again.

Emma gave him a sympathetic smile. "Then how about 'Garbage Man'?"

" 'Garbage Man,' " he repeated. "I like how that sounds. 'Willy McConnell, Garbage Man.' I'd better head on home to bed 'cause I've got to get up early in the morning." He wagged a finger at the bartender. "Make sure you get your trash out early, Earl. I'm startin' on your side of the street tomorrow." McConnell sauntered into the darkness, pride filling every step.

After a moment of silence, Earl turned his look of shock from the retreating Garbage Man to the sheriff. "Johnny, if I ever need a fence whitewashed, I know who to talk to." He gave them a wave and headed back to the bar.

Over the rumble of saloon noise, they heard his voice. "You'll never guess what the sheriff just did. He . . ."

A few moments later, a roar of laughter spilled into the darkened streets.

Emma took Barrett's arm. "Sounds like the men approved of your idea."

He straightened. "T'weren't nothin', ma'am. Just a typical twentieth-century marketing strategy. Coat it in enough glory and hype and you can sell practically anything."

Emma squeezed his arm lightly. "We doctors have the same saying. A spoonful of honey will help the medicine go down."

"Sugar," Barrett offered.

She gave him a look of mock surprise. "I beg your pardon, sir?"

"It's a spoonful of sugar. At least that's how the song goes in *Mary Poppins*."

"Who's she? A friend?"

Barrett couldn't contain his laughter. "No, she's a character in a movie."

She looked up expectantly. "And a movie is . . ."

"A motion picture. Moving pictures with sound. Like television, but in a big theater. In this case, with singing and dancing . . . and flying British nannies, penguin waiters . . ." His train of thought petered away as she leaned her head on his shoulder and released a small sigh.

"Your world must be so wonderful."

Barrett glanced at her hand tucked around his arm. In his time, women and men seldom walked so formally. The only times he'd ever had a woman hold his arm was in a posed photograph at his senior prom and when he served as best man at his college roommate's wedding.

He smiled to himself. *Now who's the best man?*

"Friends, neighbors, concerned founding fathers of Margin. I've asked for a chance to speak to you of a situation which affects you all." Alphonse Thornwald stood behind the podium which Emma knew was usually reserved for loftier pursuits such as religious instruction or mayoral proclamations. Unlike the pastor or the mayor, who both found the podium to be confining and seldom remained behind it for long, the banker gripped it with whitened knuckles. "I must admit I am mystified by your unwillingness to accept my generous offer."

"Too generous, if you ask me." Had Silas stood, it would have been a gesture of respect, but as evidenced by the grocer's slouched-in-the-pew posture, respect was the last thing on his mind.

Emma smiled to herself. It was quite a temptation to turn in the pew and sneak a glance at Barrett, but she forced herself to look at the banker.

Thornwald continued. "Do not see my offer as undue generosity. What's wrong with selling the land to a buyer who is willing to spend generously for your property rights?"

A voice echoed from the back of the church. "Who're you playing for a fool? The buyer or us?" Several townspeople chuckled, one man slapping the speaker on the back.

Thornwald swallowed with difficulty, his Adam's apple bobbing up and down nervously. "Your suspicion perplexes me to no end. Surely you realize the mine has a finite life span? The vein will not continue to produce *ad infinitum*. And when this geological phenomenon comes to a close, and I believe it *will* cease soon, you will regret not having taken advantage of my offer."

The townspeople stared at him as if he were speaking another language. Before Emma could stand and offer a translation, a familiar voice boomed from the back of the room.

"What Mr. Thornwald is trying to say is that nothing lasts forever."

Barrett looked like Johnny. He sounded like Johnny. He even stood like Johnny, something he and Emma had rehearsed several times. He ambled to the front of the room, moving with Johnny's slow, deliberate, long-legged steps.

"I think we can all agree with that, right?"

Thornwald wore a look of expectancy, as if he wasn't quite sure whether the sheriff had changed sides. When Barrett approached the podium, Thornwald yielded his position willingly, almost smiling as he stepped back.

Adopting a comfortable position at the podium, Barrett smiled at his audience. "I know each of you have listened to Mr. Thornwald's offer. And a generous one, it is. We all realize the mine will play out someday. I suppose you could say we're all gamblers of some sort."

Barrett reached into his pocket and pulled out a coin. He flipped it in the air, grabbed it, then slapped it to his wrist. "As a banker, Mr. Thornwald gambles we'll pay back our loans to him. We gamble on the mine keeping up its output." He flipped the coin again. "We gamble the price of silver will remain the same. We even gamble the sun will rise each day."

He stuffed the coin back in his pocket and turned to smile at the black-frocked pastor sitting in the front pew. "I'm sure Reverend Goodson would rather call it faith, and I think I'll join him in that. I have faith, my friends. Faith that the sun will rise each day. And even if clouds fill the sky, I have faith the sun is still there."

His voice rose a bit in pitch and volume, and Emma found herself leaning forward in the pew. Suddenly cognizant of her posture, she pulled back, but noticed others being swept up in the intoxication of Barrett's delivery.

"Faith, my friends. Pure and simple. Faith that the mine will continue to produce. Faith that the price will hold. And even faith that should the mine fail or the prices fall, then God will close one door and open another."

"Amen, brother!" An anonymous voice exploded from near the middle of the room.

Thornwald jumped forward, looking as if he wanted to wrestle the podium away from the sheriff. Barrett merely stepped back from the stand and nodded affably. "Care for a rebuttal?"

"I object!" Thornwald sputtered. "I object to the sheriff's assumption that I don't have faith in the mine and the town. I have faith. I have *faith!*" His voice rose with an ugly shrillness.

Emma caught Barrett's hooded glance and she nodded. *It's time.*

"I have faith, too, Alphonse." Barrett put extra emphasis on the name. "Faith that the Daisy Lee will prosper one way or the other. Through silver, or perhaps through another mineral which may be lurking alongside the silver vein in the darkness."

Thornwald blanched and gripped the podium so hard that Emma feared the wood might snap in two. "You paint a pretty picture, Sheriff. A mysterious metallic savior to rescue Margin?" He turned to his disgruntled audience. "Come now, you don't believe this pap, do you? Do you?"

"What I don't believe is *you*, Al-phonse." The man from the audience said the first name like a sneer. "You offered me twice as much money as my land's worth. Twice as much as you were willing to lend me last month to build a new house. It's mighty suspicious. Mighty suspicious." The man stood and made his way out to the aisle. "You can all listen to him, but I ain't gonna waste my time."

"Me, neither." The blacksmith rose.

"Or me." The newspaper editor jammed his pencil back behind his ear.

The townspeople exited in clumps, leaving occasional bursts of muted laughter behind as they emptied into the street. Thornwald remained behind the podium, no longer clutching it. He raised one fist and shook it at Barrett. "You'll be sorry you messed with me, Sheriff."

"Is that a threat?" Barrett looked anything but alarmed.

"No, a promise. When this town dies and the people look for someone to blame, you'll be the one they point to."

Barrett pivoted and headed down the center aisle. "I'll take my chances, Alphonse," he called out over one shoulder.

Emma met him halfway.

"I don't like this," Barrett whispered as they passed each other.

"We agreed . . ." Emma winked, then

moved back, raising her voice so the banker could hear. "I said please step aside. I'd like to speak to Mr. Thornwald." She shouldered past Barrett and headed toward the front of the room. "Mr. Thornwald, may I have a word with you?"

The man gave Barrett a quick look, betraying thoughts of possible triumph, however limited. Then, Thornwald smiled at Emma. "What can I do for you, Madame Schoolteacher?"

She ducked her head, trying to force a flush to her cheeks. "I just wanted to tell you that I support your efforts to help Margin. I realize how fickle—to use your own words—a 'geological phenomenon' can be. I don't understand why the sheriff is banding the townspeople against you."

Thornwald shook his head. "Ignorance. Sheer ignorance and jealousy. He may speak like an educated gentleman, but I assure you it's merely a matter of an overactive vocabulary rather than rampant intelligence."

Emma tried to appear supportive. "He is indeed silver-tongued. I heartily agree with your assessment of his intellect. Well, sir, all I wanted to do was let you know I support you. Good luck, Mr. Thornwald." She stepped away, wondering if he would take advantage of the opening gambit she'd laid at his well-polished shoes.

"Uh, Miss Nolan, wait."

She pivoted. "Yes, Mr. Thornwald?"

An oily smile slid over his face. "Please, call me George."

Emma tried to sound interested. "I thought your name was Alphonse."

He actually winced at the mention of his own name. "Alphonse is my first name. But my friends and close associates call me George."

It galled her to duck her head once more and play the simpering fool, but it was necessary. "George." She managed a proper expression of bashfulness and guarded pleasure. "My friends call me Emma."

"A lovely name for a lovely lady." He stepped closer. "Do you think I might experience the pleasure of your company? I'd like a chance to further explain my idea."

"Well . . ." she hesitated. Good sense was telling her—no, screaming at her—to run in the other direction, but she graced him with the most sincere look she could muster. "I'd like that . . . George."

"Perhaps dinner tomorrow? I might be able to bribe that bovine proprietress of the local cafe to cook up something befitting a cultured palate such as mine. Perhaps *Coq au Vin* or *Boeuf Wellington?*"

"They sound . . . intriguing. I'm sure any meal you plan would be wonderful."

He peeled back his thin lips and gave her a toothy smile which he evidently thought appeared seductive. "Until tomorrow." He snagged her hand and lifted it to his mouth. "Shall we say, seven?"

The sound of the syrupy kiss filled the town hall. Thornwald smiled again. "I do so love a woman who blushes."

Emma all but ran for the door. How dare that jackal mistake her controlled anger for anything remotely resembling passion? A blush, indeed! It had taken all her self-restraint to keep from slapping his presumptuous, smirking, leering—

"How'd it go—Whoa!" Barrett ducked as Emma's fist arced instinctively toward him. "Good heavens, Emma! You didn't deck him, did you?"

She took a deep breath, forcing her hands to her side. "Deck him? You mean hit him? No, but I wish I had." She stalked down the street, heading for the sheriff's office with Barrett trailing behind. "That man makes my skin crawl. He's insufferable, with his smarmy smile and his lascivious leer. And to think I even allowed him to *touch* me." She scrubbed the back of her hand against her skirt, trying to remove the wet imprint of his slimy lips from her skin as well as her memory.

Once she entered the office, she ripped off her bonnet and tossed it toward the desk, a gesture which had become her custom.

"Is anybody in here?" She scanned around, peering into the dark cells.

"Nope," Barrett affirmed.

"Good."

And she grabbed him.

Ten

It was a magnificent kiss which started at his lips, shot up to his brain where it toyed with his sense of balance, plunged down, pausing too long to play havoc in his pants, then shot like sparks of electricity out his toes, curling them in the process. It lasted a lifetime, or a split second; he didn't know which.

Emma pulled back suddenly, looking momentarily satisfied with herself until she realized what she had just done. She pressed her fingers against her mouth. "Oh my goodness . . ."

"Goodness . . ." Barrett hesitated. Heck, after all, Mae West was probably still in her diapers. ". . . Goodness had nothin' to do with it." He pulled her closer, hoping he could curl her toes with similar ferocity.

With one hand tangled in her silky hair and the other around her waist, he kissed her. Desire swirled around him like molten metal, burning through his self-imposed restraint. Her fingers explored his shoulders, his cheeks, his neck, each feathery touch making him lose more control.

Passion turned his voice into a graveled whisper. "No woman . . ." He shifted his kiss to her ear and she arched toward him. "has ever . . ." He slid his lips across the tender skin of her neck. "made me feel . . ." The miracle of his desire made his heart thunder. "this way . . ."

Emma threw her head back to expose the delicate flesh of her throat, which Barrett gladly sampled. She caught her breath in small, jerky gasps, and her fingers pleated the material of his shirt sleeve.

"Oh Johnny . . ."

Not me. Johnny.

The minute the words slipped from her lips, Emma tried valiantly to cover her mistake. Barrett stiffened and pulled back from her, leaving a cool breeze to dance across the moisture left from her kisses. A chill dropped over his once fevered emotions.

"Is that who you wish I was?" The words sounded almost bitter.

She reached for him, but he sidestepped her embrace.

"I'm nothing but a poor substitute for the real man of your dreams." There were no words but sardonic ones to ease his pain. The best offense against painful words was a good defense. Repartee, the sharp-edged sword of the distressed soul. "If you can't have the original, a pale copy will do?"

"No, Barrett, that's not it."

Ice edged his soul. "At least you got the name right this time."

"Please . . . don't look at me like that." She turned her head away from him, but unlike most people facing his wrath she didn't make a move to escape.

"Like what? Or should I say, like who? I suppose I should have realized that by having Johnny's face and taking Johnny's job, I could have Johnny's woman, too."

When she pivoted to face him again, a new fire of indignation flared inside her, as visible through her flashing eyes. "Johnny's woman? Is that who you think I am?" She advanced on him, stabbing an accusatory schoolteacher's finger in his chest. "I think traveling in time has scrambled your brains, Mr. Callan, or Callaghan, or whoever you call yourself. How dare you suppose that a mere physical resemblance is enough to have me swooning at your feet?"

He began to back up from her accusations as well as her finger.

"Johnny Callaghan is brave, strong, capable, and more of a man than you can ever aspire to be. And I can guarantee you he never even gave me as much as a second look as a woman. I'm the schoolmarm, the spinster left with a younger brother to raise, and therefore totally inert in his eyes. He would no more look at me as a possible love interest as he would . . . Miss Penny. And *she* can *cook!*" As soon as the words tumbled from her mouth in their uncontrolled rush, Emma realized how feeble her arguments had grown.

Emma stared at Barrett, who made no effort to disguise his confusion. Drawing a deep breath, she let it out in one big puff. "That has to be . . ." She paused, searching for the right words. ". . . the stupidest thing I have ever said."

He crossed his arms, still wearing his disconcerted expression. "I'm inclined to agree."

"You agree?" She deflated, searching for a place to support herself as her knees grew watery. "You agree to what? My assessment of the situation, or my foolishness?"

He scratched the back of his head, mimicking a gesture she'd seen his relative perform a hundred times. "I'm not Johnny Callaghan. I'm not sure why I thought I could pretend to be him." His confusion faded to dejection. "I don't think I can keep up the charade for long." He tried to smile. "At least, I can't without your continual help. Johnny . . ." He dropped into the nearest chair. "Johnny can do it all. He's the hand of justice, the voice of reason, everyone's friend and confidante. He's an expert marksman and rides horses like he was born in the saddle. Me? I think I'm hot stuff because I work out on the StairMaster three times a week and I have a gold MasterCard." He grimaced. "At least, I used to have one until I screwed up everything and the bank confiscated it."

Emma sat in the chair next to him, surprised by how deeply she shared his sense of despondency, finding a kinship in their separate failures. "I know what you mean. I had such plans to be a doctor. I'd been accepted at the University of Michigan, where I would earn a degree after a four years' medical curriculum. With my experience, they thought I might be able to get out even sooner. Then, Father lost his job in Chattanooga and he got the offer from Margin. I only planned to stay here a year, to help him and Ford settle in. Then I was going to head off to college, but all of that became history when Father died."

"I'm sorry."

She managed a halfhearted laugh. "History . . . I'm talking about history to a man from the future. I *am* history to you, aren't I? After all, Margin doesn't even exist in your time outside of a few stone foundations and a mention or two in a couple of moldy history books."

"No, you're not history to me, Emma." He reached for her face, caressing her cheek with a newly calloused thumb. "You're real, and now . . . and that scares me to death."

She touched his hand, realizing how much he'd changed since he'd arrived. Yet, through it all, she'd never thought of him as a fearful man. "You, scared? Why?"

"Because of what might happen. What *should* happen, if I set up the chain of events to change my future. If I succeed, I'll return to a new life. Back in nineteen ninety-five."

"Where Margin is history. Where I'm history."

He ran his hand through his hair. "What happens when I leave?" His voice dropped to a whisper. "What happens when I leave you behind?"

"Barrett . . ." The train of logic derailed and the new surge of emotion made her uncomfortable.

He stared across the room, his gaze unfocused. "I'll be so jealous of Johnny, back here with you."

The words sprang from somewhere deep inside her, someplace where the emotion had taken root. "But I don't love Johnny. I love you."

When he turned toward her, pain filled the vacancy in his eyes. "But Emma, I'm the one person you *can't* love. I've already started the process which will bring me back to my own time. If the people of Margin stay strong, they won't sell out to Thornwald.

At that point, I'll return to Denver in nineteen ninety-five, to what I hope is a better life for the company and for me."

"And I'll be history again." To her utter surprise, she saw what she supposed was a tear in his eye.

"No." He blinked rapidly. "You'll always be real to me. And I'll always think of what a fool I was to fall in love with the one woman I couldn't have."

She felt her own throat clogging. "Barrett . . ."

"Go home, Emma. Go back to where you really belong."

"But—"

"Go."

One part of Emma demanded she fight for the right to love him, but the other side realized the overwhelming reality of it all. This man of the future would never be allowed to stay in the past. It wasn't natural. Burdened with the heavy weight of reluctance, she stood, straightened her disheveled dress, and tried to cover her messed hair with her bonnet. Drawing one last deep breath, she glanced at him, wondering if her "brave" mask was in place.

It was the mask she'd worn at her father's funeral. The one she'd donned when formal medical training became an impossibility. The mask which protected her from the townspeople's pity.

The control Emma had dredged from within dissipated when she saw his forlorn face.

His mouth formed the word, "Go." Then, he turned away.

And she did too.

Tears and doubts filled the night. Emma had very little sleep and awoke feeling even more depressed, despite the bright welcoming sun.

Halfway through the extraordinarily long day at school, Emma remembered her supposed assignation with Alphonse Thornwald scheduled for that night. As she allowed the children to scamper out for their lunch, she called her brother to the front of the room.

"Ford." She finished scribbling a note and folded it several times. "I want you to take this note to the sheriff. Hand it to him personally, don't just leave it on his desk. If you can't find him, bring it back. And if you read this, there will be double afterschool chores for you, young man."

He puckered his face up in a pout which was exclusive to eleven-year-olds. "Ye-e-e-s, Emma." He barreled out of the room, his lunch pail flying behind him.

Emma usually ate her midday meal with a couple of the older students who claimed a shady spot under a large tree near the front steps. But that day, she ate at her desk, hoping Barrett might answer the note in per-

son. When Ford came back, still clutching
the paper in his hand, she thought perhaps
he hadn't fulfilled his quest.

Ford panted as he raced down the schoolroom aisle. "Here." He shoved the note at
her.

"Didn't find him?"

Her brother shook his head, swiping his
forehead with one sleeve. "Found him. He
wrote you a note back. Gotta go eat." He
dashed off, disappearing out the door.

Emma unfolded the paper, smoothing out
the creases. Below her message, Barrett had
scrawled, *Tonight's up to you. T. is such a sleaze
I don't really want you near him, but I need to
search for proof. You decide whether you can stand
him long enough. JBC-V.*

Emma stared at the printed words. A
"sleaze." She'd never heard the word used
before, but it painted an appropriate picture
of the slippery Thornwald. He certainly was
a "sleaze" in her opinion. How willing was
she to even pretend to like the banker? To
allow him to touch her again? She shuddered. How could she even bear the thought
of his lips touching her hand, much less any
other part of her . . .

Her traitorous mind insisted on comparing
his chilling touch to the fever which Barrett
stirred in her. She'd never initiated a kiss
before, having been on the receiving end
only a few times. But those were suitors of

her youth, little more than children themselves.

Last night, an inner desire had betrayed
her, had nearly knocked her off her feet.
Just the mere thought of the kiss filled her
with a new fever. As she attempted to savor
the moment in her memory, Barrett's scald-
ing words returned, reminding her of his
duty to his own future.

Future.

In order for him to have a future, she
would be forced to give up hers with him.
The idea of sacrifice fueled many a classic
work of literature, but in real life, it wasn't
nearly as grand or noble.

Emma stood slowly from her desk, shuffled to the back of the room, and wrapped
her fingers around the bell rope. The ring-
ing filled her ears, driving away some of the
mocking thoughts of what was not to be.

Ever.

Once the children were settled at their
desks, Emma sat down and plucked a book
off her desk. Thumbing through the pages,
she gave them the best smile she could muster.

"All right, class. It's time for a history lesson."

"You won't tell anybody about the peephole, will you, Sheriff?" Miss Penny brushed

the flour from her hands onto her apron. She shifted around the table, reminding Barrett of a ballet-dancing hippopotamus in *Fantasia*.

Barrett squinted through the hole which gave him an unobstructed view of both chairs at Thornwald's reserved table. "Your secret's safe with me, Miss Penny. As long as you keep quiet about *my* surveillance tactics."

She stared blankly at him.

"Just promise me you won't tell anybody I peeked."

"Promise." Penny made a vague crossing gesture in the general direction of her generous bosom. "I best be getting back to Mr. Thornwald's dinner. He was quite insistent about what he wanted. He even had the audacity to give me the recipe for some silly French dish." She peered into the stove and shook her head. "Why anyone would want to eat a chicken stewed on wine beats me. I had a devil of a time getting that bird to drink even half the bottle of fancy French wine he had Earl deliver earlier . . ."

Barrett camouflaged his laughter with a cough. He couldn't wait to see Thornwald's face when the man sat down to Penny's unique version of *coq au vin* . . .

When Thornwald entered the dining room, Emma had a prim hold on his arm. Her smile looked strained, the sight of which afforded Barrett great relief.

Thornwald had evidently pulled out all the stops: flowers, candy, holding doors and chairs, and wearing an insufferably proud look that Barrett wished he could knock right off the banker's pasty face.

Good manners to disguise bad intentions, Barrett's mom would say. His thoughts hesitated. *Or will say one day.*

"They're here," he whispered to Penny.

She nodded, gave her hands one last wipe on a towel, and adjusted her apron. "Here goes nothin'." She strode into the dining room, each step making the wall reverberate and tremble against Barrett's forehead. He could hear only the barest suggestion of conversation, catching just occasional words.

A few moments later, Penny returned. "Time for the wine, then the first course."

Barrett pulled his attention away from the peephole long enough to glance at her. "How many courses did he plan?"

"Seven."

Barrett permitted himself a small conciliatory smile. "Good. That gives me more time. If I'm not back by dessert, stall them. Just don't let him out of your sight!"

She nodded with enthusiasm, setting an avalanche of flesh rippling in the aftermath. "Gotcha, Sheriff."

Barrett trotted out the back door and skirted through the alley to the banker's rather lush residence. Slipping through the rear entrance, Barrett discovered a small kitchen which he immediately dismissed as a hiding place. Insufferable people like Thornwald never hid important papers in such ordinary places. Most likely, the man never even entered the room except to issue orders to his housekeeper, whom Penny assured Barrett was off for the night.

That bastard probably keeps all his secrets close at hand. Someplace like in his study.

Barrett found the shelf-lined library after the third try. The roll-top desk wasn't even locked, a fact which he eagerly grasped as an omen of impending success. Nearly an hour later, he pushed back in the chair, disgusted at his erring sense of prophecy as well as Thornwald's filing system.

Or lack thereof.

Although the man seemed to have his sticky fingers in a variety of unsavory pies, Barrett found no paperwork connected to the purchase of the Daisy Lee and surrounding properties.

The second line of offense took him to Thornwald's bedroom, where Barrett gritted his teeth and dug in. After a half hour, he gave up. Between the folded clothes, he'd found everything from French postcards of women in various modes of undress, to a copy of the *Kama Sutra*, which would be worth a veritable fortune to a late twentieth-century rare book collector. Apparently,

Thornwald believed in business in the study and whatever perverted pleasure he could find in the bedroom.

Barrett's hand froze on the doorknob. *Emma!* He'd left Emma in the company of a certifiable lecher. Barrett pounded down the steps and out the back door, praying he hadn't left too many telltale signs of a search. He almost plowed into Penny as he bolted into the boarding house kitchen.

"Penny, what's going on? Are they still there?"

She wadded her apron in her massive hands. "I tried to keep them here as long as possible, but Mr. Thornwald . . ." She almost spat his name. ". . . wanted to take Emma somewhere."

Barrett's stomach seized. He could guess to where Thornwald wanted to retire. And with whom.

"Pray for her, Miss Penny." Barrett's hand snaked unconsciously to his holster, where he was strangely reassured by the gun strapped there. "And for me, too."

He made it to Thornwald's house in record time. Skidding to a stop at the front porch steps, he paused to catch his breath. If he burst in on them, he'd have to have a good cover story. Straightening his vest, Barrett forced himself to ascend the stairs one tread at a time, rehearsing his story. "We've had a report on a prowler and I'm checking to see . . ." *Yeah, that'll work, considering some-one did break in.*

He knocked on the door.

No answer.

Wiping his sweaty palms on his pants, he knocked again. He peered through the side-lights, but saw no lights and no movement. Barrett checked the urge to do a bad imita-tion of Marlon Brando and pound on the door, yelling, "Emma!"

Where could they be?

There were no convenient yuppie hang-outs in this time period where a couple could get an after-dinner drink and admire the ferns. He seriously doubted that even Thornwald would try to take her to Margin's only watering hole, the Crystal Plume.

Where else did that leave?

Eleven

"I'm sorry to drag you away so abruptly after dessert." Thornwald gave Emma an oily smile which turned her stomach. "I would have enjoyed lingering over a liqueur and discussing the classics with you. Perhaps you can understand the impressive weight of my responsibilities as the town's only banker."

He pawed through his lap drawer, pulling out loose papers and scattering them over his desk. "If you'll bear with me for just a moment, I'll be able to turn my entire attention back to you shortly."

Emma shifted in the leather side chair and tried to look understanding. "I'm sure you wouldn't have interrupted our evening if it weren't important." She took a lace-edged handkerchief from her drawstring bag and dabbed at the back of her neck. Perhaps proper ladies weren't supposed to perspire, but tonight she hoped to play the role of a proper spy. And quite frankly, it had her in an unseemly sweat.

She tried to smile. "I didn't know the deputy was in the habit of delivering telegraph messages."

"That, my dear, was plain luck, purely and simply. Deputy Soames happened to be making his rounds and was there when the telegram came in. I'm very much indebted to him for delivering it. If I can find the figures the home office needs, then I can save them a great deal of money and make myself appear very knowledgeable in the process."

He continued to rifle through the drawer for several minutes before he whipped a handkerchief from his jacket pocket and mopped his sweating forehead. "Miss Nolan . . . Emma, dear, would you mind waiting here for a moment while I check the files in the back room?"

"Certainly. I don't mind." She offered him a brilliant smile, knowing it reflected an even more brilliant plan which Plain Luck had presented her.

As soon as she heard him enter the back room, Emma nearly sprang over the desk, and quickly began to go through the jumbled papers. Numbers filled the loose ledger sheets, along with odd notes scribbled in the margins. The gibberish meant nothing to her. Opening the lap drawer, she dug deeper, finding more useless pages containing messy columns of numbers.

He's devious, Emma! Think like him. Think . . . despicably!

Emma ran her hand beneath the drawer, instantly finding a folder stuck between the drawer and shelf. She tugged the file out and spread its contents across the desk.

Three phrases immediately jumped out at her.

Assayer's Report.

Daisy Lee.

Gold.

She drew a deep breath. "Gold . . ." she whispered. "Here? But Barrett didn't say anything about gold. Only copper." She studied the report carefully.

"Oh, there's probably copper there, too."

Emma jerked the file closed, but the figure in the doorway shook his head.

Leaning against the door frame, Thornwald made a grand gesture of crossing his arms. His unctuous expression turned from a smile to a leer. "But I'm not interested in the copper. It absolutely pales in comparison to the gold." He emitted a theatrical sigh. "I should have known. It was all a little show for my benefit, wasn't it? You and the sheriff arguing. I knew it was all a bit too convenient. So I gave you plenty of rope, and you . . ." He made a gesture of dangling from the hangman's noose. "You certainly obliged. But I have to ask . . . who's this fellow Barrett?"

Her voice surprised her with its strength and her mind with its devious turn of fantasy. "Barrett . . . is the government officer who contacted J-Johnny and warned him of your plans to swindle the townspeople of Margin. The government's been keeping an eye on your confederates back East and are ready to arrest them." She found the impetus to straighten and stare into his beady black eyes. "And arrest you, too. You might as well give up."

"Give up?" Thornwald's leer turned unexpectedly to harsh laughter. "Government men? Confederates back East? Impending arrest? Good Lord, Miss Nolan, what type of reading material do you digest? Dime novels? Brave girl detectives who talk themselves out of the dangerous grip of the evil-hearted villain?" He twirled an imaginary mustache. "Even without the appropriate props, I suppose I can still play the role of the dastardly scoundrel who cheats the town and . . ." He smiled. ". . . ravishes the heroine."

Emma stiffened as an ominous chill chased away the momentary thrill of her success. *Weapon*, her instincts shrieked. *Find a weapon*. She reached down and grabbed the handle of the drawer.

"You won't find any knives or guns in there." He took a step toward her. "I'm afraid Destiny, the real author of your little fiction, wouldn't be so considerate."

Emma waited until he came hot-breathed close before jerking the entire drawer out and slinging it in his direction. The action caught him by surprise, and he raised two hands to deflect the wooden missile. Elated by the distraction, Emma headed for the only exit from the office with a speed boosted by desperation, but Thornwald latched onto her arm as she pushed past him.

"Let go!" Emma flailed against him, surrender being an unacceptable last resort. She clawed, bit, punched, and kicked until a searing pain erupted in the back of her head and the room grew red, then black.

The bank.
Barrett figured the bank was the only other place where Thornwald might entice her to accompany him, Victorian morals being what they were.

Not morals. Curiosity. That's exactly where Emma would want to go if it meant a chance to do a little rummaging in the files behind Thornwald's back.

Barrett abandoned the back alley and moved as quickly as he could down the wooden sidewalk without gaining the undue attention of the townspeople out enjoying the unusually warm autumn evening. When he arrived at the bank, he rattled the door-knob, hoping he appeared to be doing nothing more than his normal duty as guardian of the peace.

One of the strolling couples stopped close by and the man doffed his hat.

"Evenin', Sheriff."

Barrett tried to look officious yet polite. "Nice night." *What are their names?* "Just . . . just checking to make sure everything's locked up tight."

The man smiled and nodded. "Like that skinflint Thornwald would forget to lock up his safe." He slapped Barrett on the back and began to laugh. "That's a good one, Johnny."

Barrett waited until the couple stepped away before heading around to the back of the building. From the alley side, the bank's windowsills started about a foot above his head. A neat pile of trash waited for McConnell's morning trash pickup, providing Barrett with a wooden crate to drag beneath the window. Standing on the box, he peered into the bank.

It looked as if a tornado had swept through the room; papers were strewn across the desk and floor, a drawer emptied out and propped against the door. Barrett used his sleeve to remove a layer of grime from the window, hoping to see more.

He spotted what he didn't want to see beneath the leg of the overturned chair.

A woman's bag.

Emma's.

Barrett drew a shuddering breath, leaned against the building, and slid down the wall, ending up in a squat. He used every elaborate invective he knew to curse the sum total of his stupidity, his errant sense of invincibility, his fallible presumption that a mere knowledge of the future placed him higher in the intellectual food chain than nineteenth-century man.

Emma.

His stomach tightened, his fists, too.

Where could she be? What had Thornwald done? What would he be likely to do?

Don't jump to conclusions, Barrett. Maybe she's all right. Maybe . . . maybe . . . "Maybe I don't know jack shit . . ." he spoke aloud.

One small thought began to glimmer in his mind, providing the only beacon for him to follow.

But I know someone who can tell me . . .

He tore into the darkness, following instinct.

Less than a minute later, Barrett burst through the door into his room in the boarding house and paused only long enough to catch his balance. He stood in front of the oak washstand, still heaving for breath.

"Johnny! I know you're in there."

His reflection screamed at him, echoing his words of panic.

"You've got to come back, Johnny. I . . . I need you. Emma needs your help."

He saw only the image of a desperate man.

"God damn you, Johnny. Emma needs . . . needs you, not me."

The door burst open and Harvey Kirk thundered into the room. "What are you doing? The whole building can hear you." He stared at Barrett, then gripped the door, shoving it closed behind him. "Good Lord! What happened?"

Barrett recited the painful litany of details, the plans made in rampant ignorance and their dangerous outcome. He grabbed Harvey's shoulders and peered into the face creased with concern. "Johnny. We need Johnny. He'll know what to do."

Harvey knocked away Barrett's hands. "Get a grip, mister. Johnny's not coming back. He can't. You're going to have to deal with this yourself." He reached into his pocket and handed Barrett a piece of folded paper. "I found this stuck on your office door."

Sheriff,
    I assume it's evident to you that I have a package you might like to bargain for. It's surprising what power a man like you can wield

*with a few well-chosen words to the right ears.
I believe we can agree on a trade, my package
for your support of my plan to purchase the
land. Make no effort to find us; you wouldn't
be pleased with the outcome, should I feel pres-
sured. Meet me at my office in the morning
at 10:00, where I expect to receive your total
cooperation.*

Alphonse Thornwald

Barrett felt rage boil up inside him as he
read the words. "He's got her. That bastard
has Emma." The paper crumpled in his fist.
"If he so much as musses her hair, I'll tear
him into a thousand pieces."

Harvey crossed his arms. "You'll have to
find him first."

"Find him . . ." Barrett tossed the wad of
paper at the mirror. "How the hell can I
find him? Where could he have taken her?"

"Well, the obvious places are out. Thornwald's intelligent. He'll stay away from his
place or the bank."

A bitter ripple of laughter escaped from
Barrett. "That only leaves the rest of Colorado to search. The rest of the world."

"No it doesn't, you fool. He won't go far."
A gleam started in Harvey's eye. The corner
of his mouth twitched up. "But I bet he's
gone deep."

Comprehension dawned. "The mine . . .
of course. Tomorrow's Sunday and opera-

tions will be shut down. He'll have the place to himself." Barrett ground one fist into the opposite palm, wishing it was Thornwald's face. The sun of awareness rose higher in his conscience, lighting a harsh reality. "My God . . . the mine." A lead weight of dread dropped on his chest, making him draw a ragged breath. "I can't . . . I can't go down there."

Harvey stared at him. "Why not?"

"Because . . ." Barrett couldn't say the words. He could feel the sensations, relive the agony of his crushing fears, but he couldn't bring himself to describe them aloud.

"Don't chicken out on me now, Callaghan." Harvey raised an eyebrow, giving Barrett a harsh glare.

"Callan," he corrected automatically.

"No, you left your other identity behind when you came here." Harvey pointed to the mirror. "Through there, back in the twentieth century, Barrett Callan was a royal screwup. But here, as Johnny, you're making a difference."

"A difference? Like putting Emma in danger? Yeah." Barrett dropped to the bed, pleating the thin bedspread between his white-knuckled grips. "If I'm making such a difference, why haven't I returned to a new future? I've convinced the people they shouldn't sell. What more am I supposed to do?"

"If I were you, I'd start with saving Emma."

"But how . . ."

"Use your head, you idiot. You know all about those mine shafts, whether you've ever been down there or not."

Barrett felt a kernel of begrudging acceptance form in the knot of his stomach. "I've studied the maps since I was a child. I went down there . . . once, for fifteen minutes, before I almost passed out."

Harvey nodded with encouragement. "Then you should be able to figure out exactly where Thornwald might try to hide underground."

"Yeah . . ." Barrett thought back to the sound of the scratchy ink pen. "And I know Thornwald's familiar with the tunnel layout. He sketched a map of the Daisy Lee for me, and it was accurate. Damned accurate."

"So if he knows the mine well . . ." Harvey abandoned his post by the door and dragged a chair across the room. He straddled it backward and propped his chin on the back of the chair. "Then it's an even likelier place to hide. Where do you think he'd have her?"

Barrett massaged his temples, trying to jump-start brain functions shut down by panic. "There are three main branches. 'Forty Crawl,' 'High Country,' and 'Widow Maker.'" He paused. Something was wrong with his historical timing. "Wait . . . it wasn't named 'Widow Maker' until the cave-in of nineteen-oh-nine. Before that it was . . ." He allowed himself a ragged breath. "They used to call it 'Lucky Lady.' "

He shook himself, trying to get past the unpleasant symmetry of events. "But 'High Country' passes through a natural cavern. We used to use it for storage . . . mining bits, water pump parts, even a stockpile of civil defense supplies. If I were Thornwald, I'd hole up there. Plenty of space, relatively dry, easily defensible. They say the acoustics there are perfect, providing a sort of early warning system."

"Sounds like a good setup."

"For him. Not me. I don't know how I'll get there without him hearing me." The moment after he spoke, Barrett realized he'd already accepted the fact that he was going underground.

Into the bowels of the deep, dark earth.

The absolute darkness in an era without flashlights.

In a place where the mythology of countless cultures had placed the fires of Hell. Fire might provide illumination in the darkness, but you had to be dead to appreciate the view.

He wiped his sweaty palms on his pant leg, commanding his heart rate to drop out of warp speed.

"Just take a deep breath, hold it, then release it in small puffs," Harvey offered.

Barrett closed his eyes and nodded. After the last puff, he sighed, feeling marginally better. "Where'd you learn that technique?"

The man grinned. "From Lamaze class. I've got two grown kids. Take it from me—at least, take it from my wife—that natural childbirth stuff really works." He leaned forward. "Are you going to be all right? With going underground . . . I mean."

Barrett nodded. "I have to be. Emma's life depends on it. And my future, too."

"You're right." Harvey pulled his watch out of his vest pocket and reached into its face. "Lessee . . ." He appeared to be having a hard time fishing something out. He gave Barrett an apologetic shrug. "I've got too much stuff in here . . . ah, there it is." He pulled out a small flashlight and handed it to Barrett.

"What's this for?"

"For you. It's a light."

"But I thought you said the watch didn't work that way. That it couldn't produce anything for me to use."

"It's not supposed to, but . . . my brother-in-law tinkered with it a little during my last visit home. You know . . . for my mom's birthday party?" He held up the thin aluminum tube. "As soon as you turn the flashlight on, you've got an hour's worth of juice." He leaned forward and his eyebrows drew together in concern. "But listen carefully . . . this is vitally important. Once the power source approaches the last stages, the light'll start blinking. Get rid of it before the third blink. Throw it as far away from you as you can."

"Why?"

"Because it'll explode. We've elongated the flashlight's life span outside of the temporal field, but by doing that, we compressed the final destabilization to a nanosecond implosion. Whatever you do, don't be touching it after that third blink."

Barrett turned the metal canister over in his hands, trying to view the innocent-looking cylinder as lethal. "A combination flashlight and hand grenade." He swallowed hard. "What will they think of next . . ."

"Be careful." Harvey backed toward the door.

"Wait a minute, Harvey." The familiar fingers of fright began to tighten around Barrett's throat, again. "Aren't you coming with me?"

"I can't." The man shrugged. "It's Saturday night. I've got to go back."

"Back?" Barrett's astonishment faded to sarcasm. "What is it? Poker night with the boys?" The uncontrolled irony in his tone tasted bad. The second after he spoke, regret hit in full force. "I'm sorry . . . that was uncalled for."

"Forget it . . ." A strained smile appeared on Harvey's face for a moment. He glanced at his pocket watch, which had again adopted a mundane clock face. "I've pushed the edges of the envelope already because I thought you'd get the goods on Thornwald and I wanted to be here to celebrate. I should have been back an hour ago." He ran a forefinger around the neck of his shirt, loosening his collar. Visible drops of perspiration dotted his forehead.

"Harvey, are you going to be all right?" Barrett gripped his friend's arm.

The man nodded. "Just as soon as I get back to my own time. It'll take me three full hours to reestablish complete temporal stability, but I'll get back here as soon as possible after that. I promise." Harvey clasped Barrett's forearm. "Good luck, buddy."

"I'll need it."

"You don't think Barr . . . er, Johnny will be so foolish as to come by himself?" Emma tugged at the rope which pinned her to the chair. The cavern echoed her words, mimicking her bravery and making her sound weak and foolish.

Thornwald offered her a smile which glittered in the halo of the kerosene lamp. "As a matter of fact, I'm counting on it. You see . . ." He squatted and began to unwind the wire from the spool. "I've studied men like him. The quintessential lone wolf who occupies a position of power. I've violated his narrow code of ethics, and his first re-action will be to come storming in here with the sole purpose of rescuing you, his lady love. He won't stop to plan his strategies. He'll act merely to satisfy that animalistic part in him which demands instant retribu-tion. My little jibe about receiving his answer in the morning was calculated to push him into premature action."

Thornwald stopped long enough to hold his pocket watch up to the light. "And I ex-pect he'll be here within the half hour. Par-don me if I don't have time to explain it all to you." He continued to fiddle with the wire until he suddenly stood and brushed the dirt from the knees of his pants. "There. All done. All I need now is one knight er-rant." He picked up the lamp and crossed the cavern in a few long strides. "And now for you, my dear." He smiled again. "I do so like playing this role of the Evil Master-mind. I get to say such malicious lines and do such villainous deeds."

"You're mad . . ."

He began to clap. "Yes! Now you're in the spirit of things. Your next line should be 'You'll never get away with this, you fiend!' "

He pulled a handkerchief out of his pocket. "I'm so glad we have the same taste in tawdry literature."

Emma fought him as he attempted to stuff the material in her mouth, but he clamped an iron grip around her throat, squeezing until she surrendered. He produced a second piece of material which he tied behind her head, holding the gag in place.

"There." He dimmed the lamp to the barest glow. "Now we wait. Sir Galahad should arrive at any moment."

Barrett clutched the saddle horn with both hands, trying to find a rhythm which complemented the horse's gait.

Pretend it's a motocross bike, he kept reminding himself. Although he'd never ridden anything remotely resembling a motorcycle, it seemed to be an apt analogy from the next century. Barrett understood the rudiments of navigation and managed to aim the horse in the direction of the mine at a reasonable pace.

But any faster, and he wouldn't be able to think.

His first plan of attack fizzled when he realized the air shaft he'd planned to climb down wouldn't be drilled until the late 1920s. On second thought, he was just as glad not to attempt unaccompanied rappelling for the first time. Another case of understanding the basics without ever having performed the task.

Left with no other strategy than a frontal assault, Barrett allowed himself one long sigh when he spotted the outcropping entrance to the mine. The moon donated some unnecessary atmosphere by draping the landscape with long shadows, making the harmless look harmful and the dangerous look downright lethal. He tied the horse to the rail by the foreman's shack and pulled off the saddlebag of supplies.

He felt like Rambo, loaded down with Johnny's heavy gun, an extra bandolier of ammunition, a hank of rope, two knives, and the explosive flashlight.

This is ridiculous.

After he pared down his artillery, he had the gun, a pocketful of extra bullets, and the smaller of the two knives stuck in his boot.

And, of course, his killer flashlight.

Barrett paused at the mine entrance, sent up a prayer of contrition, and stepped into the yawning mouth of terror-inducing darkness.

Seven steps into the shaft, his throat began to close. He imagined the stale air growing thin and the ceiling straining against the crossbeams highlighted in the narrow beam from the flashlight.

Ten thousand tons of rock held up only by a four-by-four beam . . .

No steel pinning rods.

No OSHA inspectors prying into safety practices.

I'm going to die . . .

Barrett forced himself to take another step. Then another. Falling into a rhythm, he began to synchronize his breathing with his steps.

Inhale, step, step, step, exhale, step, step, step.

His heart decided to join in and stop racing ahead at breakneck speed. Just as he thought the fear was abating, he heard a noise which started the maelstrom up again.

Ahead, a pair of eyes shone in the darkness, reflecting the beam of the flashlight. He could hear a strange panting sound ahead of him. His hand snaked its way down to the gun and tightened around the grip, independent of any direct request from Barrett's conscious thought.

Suddenly, he heard movement and something furry streaked past his leg. The gun barrel never cleared the holster.

Dog? His stomach lurched. *Wolf?* He drew a shaky breath. Whatever it was, it was gone. Time to press on. He made the turn into the left branch of the mine, heading toward the cavern.

He measured his progress by landmarks.

As a kid, he'd made up for his inability to go underground by grilling the foreman and others about every detail of the mine. All his life he'd been waiting for the moment he would be allowed to step into the mine and see its wondrous sights for himself.

Sixteen, his father had promised. He could go in when he was sixteen. And on his sixteenth birthday, the first day of summer vacation, he took the elevator down the mine shaft.

And suffered a grand mal panic attack.

Sixteen years later . . . or eighty-six years earlier—however a time-traveler measured time—here he was.

Finally.

Barrett recognized each signed cross brace, carved with the initials of the miners who slaved in the darkness. By his time, records with their names had been destroyed or lost, but now Barrett knew some of the names to put to the once anonymous initials.

RH
Reuben Helms
PB
Paul Blaylock
QL
He knew the cavern was only four crossbeams ahead. He switched off the flashlight, hoping to save its waning illumination. The moment the light vanished, the familiar dread began to build in him, but somehow,

Barrett found new strength in his desire to rescue Emma from whatever fate Thornwald had planned for her.

Barrett gulped back his panic.

I got her into this, I have to get her out.

He touched the cold, damp wall of stone, feeling a cautious path through the total darkness. The shaft narrowed, then angled to the left. The darkness lost its absolute quality and Barrett began to see the barest glimmer penetrating the inky blackness.

His muscles relaxed, his breathing subsided to the minimum, and his heart rate slowed to a crawl. His eyesight sharpened as the light turned the blackness to shades of gray.

He spotted the wire first, placed just an inch or so above the mine floor. A trip wire or an early warning device? Either way, Barrett stepped over it cautiously, narrowly missing another wire which was evidently a back-up system.

Two booby traps down. How many more to go?

The mine angled back to the right. Once he made the turn, Barrett could see a vague glow outlining the entrance to the cavern. A familiar chill crept up his back, and he stopped.

It was a boardroom-honed instinct which usually signaled a carefully laid trap. But the usual business pitfalls were a matter of deceptive words and misleading numbers. But whether it was a verbal knife in his back or a real gun aimed at his head, Barrett sensed new danger.

Listening carefully, he could hear the rhythmic *plink* of water hitting rock. He studied the relative silence between the drippy echoes, picking up the undertones of another sound emanating from the cavern. Someone breathing.

Emma or Thornwald? Or both?

Wiping his palm quietly on his shirt, he reached down for the gun strapped to his leg. The weapon felt incredibly light, like a mere extension of his hand. Backing up against the mine wall, he inched toward the opening, not knowing quite what he'd do when he got there. Imitating every war movie and cop show he'd ever seen on television, he peered cautiously into the cavern, gun pointed up.

The kerosene lamp back-lit the figure in the chair, but it was a welcomely familiar silhouette. Ah, but it was a typical setup, and he wasn't going to rush in and fall for the dangling bait, even if that bait was Emma.

Barrett lowered to one knee and scanned the area, searching the shadows. Thornwald was there . . . somewhere, Barrett was sure of that, immersed in the darkness and waiting for Johnny Callaghan's bold move.

Not Barrett Callan's tentative one.

A wooden crate placed a few feet from the cavern wall created convenient coverage to the left of the entrance. Barrett slipped into the shadows behind the box, praying he made no telltale sounds. Acoustics would be his enemy here, pinpointing his position by the magnified echoes. Inching along the wall, he decided to circumnavigate the chamber, perhaps avoiding whatever booby trap Thornwald had planned next.

He heard a muffled sound and froze. Although he was sure the noise came from Emma, the cavern walls had distorted the reverberation and made it seem as if it were coming from a dozen competing directions. Thornwald could be anywhere, ready to take a potshot at anything that moved.

So, give him a target.

Barrett slipped the flashlight out of his pocket, shielded the end, then turned it on. He had no idea how much juice the thing had left in it, but he had time to wait for it to start blinking. At the moment, he needed a loud diversion like a grenade more than he needed a flashlight.

After fifteen minutes, the light began to weaken.

Then it blinked.

Barrett gripped the cylinder, feeling a sudden rush of panic. Harvey hadn't told him how much time there was between blinks.

Were they one right after the other? Or was there a lag time between them?

Don't take any chances! Get rid of—

He threw.

It hurtled through the air with the precision of a well-kicked football heading for the perfect spot between the goal posts. Its trajectory would take the flashlight over Emma's head and far across the room, protecting her from its explosive repercussions, but halfway through the arc, the room reeled with an eruption. The flashlight spun out of control and fell at Emma's feet.

And then it blinked again.

Twelve

Barrett didn't have time for conscious thought. However, his subconscious mind devised three different ways he could die by the time he hurdled the box and zigzagged a post pattern to Emma.

Death by bullet: *Thornwald would make a helluva Olympic skeet shooter.*

Death by temporal instability: *Set phasers on kill.*

Death by falling rock: *And the walls came tumblin' down.*

Barrett dove to the dirt, came up with the flashlight, slung it toward the wall, and tackled Emma, chair and all, hoping to protect her from the impending explosion. He heard the breath go out of her as they hit the unyielding stone floor of the cavern to the sound of splintering wood. The metallic zing of bullets and the puffs of dust near his face reminded him that there were still at least two fingers of Death pointing at him.

Thornwald rose like a specter, smoking gun in one hand and flashlight in the other.

The caverns still echoed with the whine of ricocheted shots. The banker smiled.

"See, Miss Nolan? Your hero made his dramatic attempt to rescue you." His expression turned thoughtful. "But I must say I've never seen anything like this light stick before. Where in the world did you get it, Sheriff?"

Barrett ignored him, trying to shift off Emma and make sure she'd survived the fall. "Emma . . ." He pulled off her gag.

Although dazed, she nodded. "I'm all right."

"Stay down." He took a step toward the man. "You'd better—"

Thornwald shifted, smirking again. "No, you'd better . . ."

Barrett stared down a gun barrel which suddenly looked like the bore of a cannon. He stepped back and raised his hands, offering what he hoped appeared as a nonthreatening gesture. "Be careful with that thing. It's likely to go off."

"That's what guns are for, Sheriff. To dispatch the unwanted."

"Not the gun, stupid, the—" Before Barrett could finish, the flashlight began to glow.

Thornwald screamed in pain, dropped the metal cylinder, and stepped back from it. Wedged in a piece of rock, the flashlight bathed Thornwald in a circle of harsh light. The silvery tube began to vibrate, then turned red. Barrett dragged Emma to her feet, heedless of Thornwald's shrieks.

She struggled against the rope which still bound her hands. "What's happ—"

"No time." Barrett pulled her toward the exit. Only a few paces away, they heard a bloodcurdling screech, and the force of a vacuum pulled them backward, almost off their feet.

The rumbling noises behind them drowned out his warning. *"Run!"*

Somehow, he was able to lead them through the lightless passageway without either getting them lost or remembering his debilitating fears of the dark depths beneath tons of crushing rocks. When they saw the silvery gleam of outside light, they both broke into a run.

Once in the blessed moonlight, Emma turned a fearful face back to the mine entrance. "Do you think . . ."

Barrett felt oddly solemn. "No one could have survived that."

She looked back at him, a tear tracking down her dust-streaked features. "Oh Barrett . . ." Burying her face against his shirt front, she began to shake with sobs.

The hot moisture soaked through his shirt. Wrapping his arms around her, he held her, muttering comforting things and wishing he could release his own tension in a similar manner. After a few moments, Emma looked up with red-rimmed eyes and kissed him all too briefly.

She snuffled, then gave him a drippy smile. "Can you do me a favor?"

He brushed back the hair which clung to her damp cheek. "Anything."

"Would you untie my hands?"

He allowed himself to laugh, finding it to be as much of a release as her tears were for her. "Sure. Turn around." His laughter faded when he stared at the rough rope twisted around her wrists. The knots defied definition, much less unraveling. "I don't know where he learned to tie. Certainly not in the Boy Scouts."

She tried to glance over her shoulder at his task. "What are 'boy scouts'?"

"They're . . . oh, never mind. It's not important. I'm just lucky to have a knife." He reached down to his boot top and drew the blade from its leather sheath. "Let me just . . ." He watched her fists clinch and her knuckles grow suddenly white. "Emma, what's wrong?" As soon as he glanced at her face, he knew. Barrett pivoted and drew a sharp involuntary breath at the sight.

Thornwald's elegant suit had been reduced to tatters. He cradled his left hand to his chest, his injury swathed in ragged strips of bloody material. Unfortunately, his right hand still held the gun, which wavered in their direction.

Still camouflaged by Emma, Barrett pushed the hilt of the knife into her fingers. "Sssshh," he cautioned, stepping around her. "It's all over, Alphonse."

"George!" the man screamed in a shrill voice. "You'll call me George . . ." He paused, pain, fear, and unchecked greed combining into madness in his eyes. "No, you'll call me Mister Thornwald. You'll call me that name with respect before you die." He maneuvered his injured hand into what was left of his jacket and pulled out a tattered piece of paper, which he allowed to flutter to the ground. Brandishing the gun with better aim, he licked his cracked lips. "Pick up that paper. Slowly."

Barrett reached down and retrieved the paper, continuing to keep his attention on the man's trigger finger. The paper had survived the blast about as well as the banker had, singed around the edges but mostly intact. Barrett stared at it.

Legal terms had changed somewhat through the years, but he recognized the document as a partnership contract, detailing one Johnny Callaghan as an authorized purchasing agent for Continental Consortium.

Barrett pointed to the paper. "Aren't you missing something? Isn't this supposed to be the Continental Silver and Copper Consortium?"

"Copper?" The man released a near-maniacal

laugh. "That's a good one." He aimed the gun toward Emma. "Sign it or I'll shoot her."

"Don't do anything hasty, Al—Mr. Thornwald. I'll sign. But you could at least explain why."

"It's simple. When the townspeople find your body in the mine, they'll find this very curious document in their beloved sheriff's pocket, revealing how he galvanized the townspeople against me merely so he could swindle the property from them himself. I'm afraid your posthumous reputation won't be worth much."

"But the people won't believe Emma had anything to do with this."

Thornwald glanced at her. "No, they won't. But they *will* believe she was your innocent pawn. Sign it, if you don't want her to meet the same fate as yours."

Barrett heaved what he hoped appeared to be a sigh of defeat. He held out his left hand. "But I don't have a pen."

Mottled red splotches colored the banker's pale face. "You'll sign it in blood if you have to!" Thornwald pawed his shirt and held out a pencil stub in his injured hand. The gun swung toward Barrett again. "Don't even think about trying something rash. I was an expert marksman at Yale. Class of eighty-one."

"No, Barrett." Emma called from behind

him. "Don't sign it. He's going to kill me anyway."

Thornwald shook with rage. "Shut up, you little—"

Barrett shifted, trying to stand between Emma and the unsteady gun barrel. "Don't. I'll sign."

"I knew you would." A triumphal gleam grew in the man's eyes.

The second that the sense of triumph seemed to split Thornwald's attention, Barrett reacted. He reached out and, instead of grabbing the pencil, he seized Thornwald's hand. Squeezing the bandaged palm, he jerked the man off balance. The banker let out an injured roar which intensified when Barrett performed a perfect left-footed goal-winning kick aimed at Thornwald's gun hand. The weapon skidded off into the scrub oak.

A second kick made a perfect high arc and connected with Thornwald's head. He screamed and dropped to his knees. Barrett reached down and regained his leverage on the banker's hand, flexing the injured wrist past its normal angle. Thornwald's florid face rapidly returned to its original pasty shade as he writhed in obvious agony, trying to lessen the pressure on his hand. "I y-yield."

Barrett released him.

Thornwald's face twitched, and he melted

to an ungainly position on the ground. After a moment, he struggled to speak. "That k-kick . . . W-where did you learn to p-play As-association Football?"

Barrett allowed himself his own perverted sense of triumph, unable to prevent himself from smiling. "Harvard. Intramural League. Most Valuable Player in eighty-three and eighty-four."

He watched the man's eyes close. "And at Hah-vahd, we call it 'soccer.' "

Emma bounced her stare from her rescuer to her former captor, fighting the urge to imitate Barrett's kicking maneuver on the now-unconscious man. When she turned her attention back to her hero, Barrett gave her a charming, if strained, smile and cleared his throat.

"I have a feeling that if I untied you right now, your hands would go around his throat." Despite his words to the contrary, he took the knife from her and began to saw through the ropes.

"You're right." She massaged the welts left by the ropes and glared at Thornwald, who shuddered. "I wish you could teach me how to kick like that."

"I can if you really want to learn." Barrett returned the knife to his boot. "I was taught by a real master of the game, an exchange student from Liverpool where they play a slightly more aggressive version of soccer. I think it's considered a blood sport in England."

He stared at her, a look of extreme gentleness on his face. "Are you all right? Really all right?" He ran a thumb down her cheek, stroking her skin softly.

The words clogged her throat, then exploded in a sob. "I am . . . now." Heedless of the pain in her hands, she threw her arms around him, wondering if she'd ever let go. She felt his hands caress her hair and heard his ragged sigh echo in the silence.

After a moment, he spoke softly. "When I saw your bag in his office, and the mess . . . I just wanted to find him and kill him."

His chaste kiss on her forehead broke the dam which held back her emotions. Their second kiss allowed her to take the strength of her fears and transform them to a thought-consuming passion. Never had she imagined herself feeling any emotion with such ferocity. Her head whirled with the intensity as her dreams and reality merged. Barrett's hold on her tightened when her knees grew watery.

"Em?"

"Don't stop," she muttered, wanting the sensation to last forever.

"Emma, we have to do something. About him." Barrett nodded toward the form crumpled on the ground. "We can't just leave him there."

"Why not? That's exactly what he was going to do to us. Except he was going to kill us first."

Barrett stepped back and gave her a puzzled smile. "This is a new side of you, Emma." His grin widened. "I think I like it." He gave her one more smoldering kiss, then broke away with a sigh. He glared at Thornwald. "All I need is some rope." He turned around and scanned the supplies attached to his horse's saddle. "We'll hogtie Sleeping Beauty here and ride back to town the conquering hero."

"And heroine," she prompted. No longer a captive, Emma became a doctor once more. She dropped to her knees beside Thornwald and felt for his pulse.

"And heroine," Barrett repeated. He pivoted, and spotted her administering to the injured man. "Wait a minute . . . first you give me the bloodthirsty 'leave him to the elements' routine, and now you're playing the Good Physician? You surprise me, Emma." He knelt down beside her and gave her patient a critical once-over. "Help me roll him over. I don't trust the bastard."

"Wait a minute." She gave Thornwald a cursory examination, determining he'd survived his ordeal at Barrett's hands . . . and feet. She helped roll the banker over. "Be careful. I think his wrist is broken."

Barrett nodded. "Then we'll just splint

it . . . with his other arm." In a few minutes
they had Thornwald sufficiently trussed, ren-
dering him no threat either to them or to
his own injuries. They dragged him into the
foreman's shack and exited in time to watch
the fingers of dawn pull at the midnight fabric of the sky, drawing it aside for the sun.

Emma gaped at this new poetic side to her
soul; she guessed falling in love did that to
a woman. She stared into the waning night.
"Do people still make a wish on the first
star they see . . . in your time?"

"Still do." Barrett slipped an arm around
her shoulders. "It's funny. I had that same
thought soon after I got here."

She could feel his arm stiffen. "You'll go
back soon, won't you? After all . . . the people won't sell to Thornwald now."

"I guess so. I don't really have any control
over it."

"You mean, one moment you could be here
and the next, you could just disappear?"

He shrugged. "I suppose it could happen
that way. Or maybe one minute I'm Barrett
and the next . . . it's Johnny standing next
to you."

Emma tried to smile. "He'd be awfully
surprised to find himself standing next to
me . . . like this." She leaned her head
against his shoulder, drawing an immeasur-
able amount of comfort from his proximity.

Barrett placed one finger beneath her chin

and tipped her face up to meet his. "Or like this." A sad passion filled their kiss, almost as if they were expecting it to be their last. Emma wondered if, at the end, she would pull back and see a puzzled face—Johnny's face—staring at her in total shock.

When they did finally break apart, she kept her eyes closed, unwilling to watch the change.

"Emma . . ." His voice was soft, cajoling.

She cracked open one eye.

He wore a strained smile. "It's still me."

They rode back in silence.

Barrett suffered mixed feelings, wondering why he hadn't returned to the twentieth century, yet feeling glad he still remained in the past. After a while, Emma stopped turning around to see if it was still "Barrett" holding her.

She urged the horse over a rocky passage, evidently aware of his lack of riding skills. "You don't like horses, do you?"

He smiled. He would gladly have given her the reins when they first mounted, but it took a few stumbles and slips before he surrendered the animal's control to her. "I think it's a matter of horses not liking me. I do all right with pets, like dogs and cats, but not with major livestock."

"You're what we call a 'city slicker.' They

probably don't use that term in the twentieth century."

He sighed. "First . . . yes, they do still use 'city slicker' in my day, and second, the twentieth century isn't some far distant future for you. It's only a little over eight years from now."

"You're right." She paused, clucking at the horse. "But you have less time than that to reach the twenty-first century. That's still the 'far distant future' to me."

Barrett took a moment to digest her words. "It's scary, isn't it? The dawn of a new century? I have a hard enough time remembering to write the new year on my checks in January. Think how odd it will be to put down *twenty* instead of *nineteen.*"

She nodded. "Or to write *nineteen* instead of *eighteen.*"

He tightened his arm around her. "Touché."

The sun rose high enough to make the tin roofs of the town shine white as if they were covered with snow.

Winter in Margin.

He probably wouldn't stay around long enough to see it. No arctic wind to chill the bones, no drifts up to the eaves . . . no Emma by the fireplace, sharing a quilt with him.

Barrett straightened, trying to force the traitorous thoughts out of his mind.

You can't stay.

He wondered if it was his own conscience speaking the words or Johnny's voice in his mind. He woke from his reverie, feeling the reins being stuffed back into his hand. They were at the edge of town.

"I'm just a passenger, remember?" Emma whispered.

Barrett had managed to steer the horse to the rail outside his office, and was in the middle of a clumsy dismount, when Jimmie Soames rushed out.

"Sheriff! We were about to ride out and search for you." Jimmie reached out, offering Emma a hand down from the horse. "Miss Emma . . . are you all right, ma'am? The town's been worried sick about you. Especially Ford."

For one fleeting second, Barrett wanted to shoulder the man aside. The strength of this unexpected streak of jealousy took him by complete surprise. Emma gave him a strained smile, then accepted Jimmie's assistance. Barrett forced himself to step back and waited patiently until she had dismounted.

Before he could say anything, Ford burst out of the front door of the boarding house and barreled down the sidewalk toward them. "Emma!"

Barrett stepped aside in time to prevent a collision. He watched the young boy attach himself to his sister's waist and try to hide his tears.

"When you didn't come home . . . I was so scared."

Miss Penny thundered down the walk behind her young charge. "Gracious saints have mercy! You're back!"

As she lumbered toward them, Barrett braced himself, waiting to be caught in her smothering cleavage. To his utter surprise, she stiff-armed him out of the way and went right to Emma. "You poor babe, tell me that vile man didn't put . . . oh my goodness. Your *hands!*" Penny pushed back the sleeves which covered the worst of Emma's injuries.

Even Barrett paled at the bruises which mottled the skin around her wrists.

Penny wedged herself between Emma and him. "You handle all that legal folderol, Sheriff, while I take this poor child back to my place and treat her." Penny pushed Emma toward the boarding house. "Now, Emma, I know you're the doctor around here, but you can't bandage this yourself. Come on, Ford . . ."

Like an anxious puppy, the boy trailed the two women back to the boarding house, leaving Barrett with Jimmie.

Jimmie grabbed the horse's reins and deftly twisted them around the hitching post. "Well, tell me what happened."

Barrett stretched, crediting his stiffness to

either the explosion, the fight, or the ride home.

"Jimmie . . ." He paused, then gave the deputy a tired smile. "Let's talk . . . over a drink."

His deputy looked alarmed. "But it's only morning! Saloon don't open until noon."

Barrett unstrapped his holster and shoved it into the hands of his unsuspecting assistant. He pointed to the dusty badge still pinned to his vest. "What's the use of authority if I can't throw my weight around every now and then. To the Crystal Plume! And the first round's on me."

Thirteen

"No, we ain't gonna play 'Clementine' again!" The band leader leaned down from his makeshift stand and shouted at an insistent patron. "I'm tired of seein' you cry into your beer." He turned back to his ragged group of musicians. "C'mon boys, let's do the march."

The band struck up an off-key, yet enthusiastic, version of the "Washington Post March." Barrett scanned the Crystal Plume, wondering how such an elaborate event could be organized and instituted in the matter of one day.

He winced at an enthusiastic cymbal crash.

And why does the guest of honor have to be so close to the band?

Red, white, and blue bunting draped the balcony, and the moose head. Since this celebration had been deemed a family event, the "ladies" had retired upstairs. Barrett could see only their slippered toes below and ribbon-festooned heads above the decorations.

What he couldn't see, the imagination glee-
fully provided.

But this was no time to idly admire mer-
chandise he had no intention of ever purchasing.

Where was Emma?

He knew he should be embarrassed about
his succession of thought, but the thought or
sight of any woman just made him think
more about Emma. He scanned the room
impatiently, cursing the launderer who'd put
enough starch in his collar to keep it upright
in a gale-force wind. Barrett looked down
and straightened the star badge pinned to
Johnny's Sunday-best brocade vest.

He discovered Ford holding court in a corner of the room, evidently keeping a group
of classmates spellbound with his version of
recent events. Emma still hadn't arrived. She
had been spirited off by Penny after their
triumphal return, and Barrett hadn't seen
either of the women since. His time had
been spent arranging Thornwald's incarcera-
tion and dealing with all the legal entangle-
ments therein. Barrett knew he wouldn't
really enjoy himself until she arrived at the
party.

And it was quite a party.

The bar looked as if it should sag under
the weight of the food. Lemonade replaced
whiskey, but much to Barrett's relief, the
beer still flowed.

Someone slapped him on the back and shoved a fresh mug in his hand. "Now, tell me how you got away from . . ."

Barrett launched into the abbreviated version of his adventures, which neglected to mention the flashlight from hell and a few award-winning soccer kicks. In the midst of the recitation, he spotted Harvey hurrying into the bar. Barrett quickly wrapped up his story and excused himself. He gestured across the room at his fellow time-traveler, and they both headed for an unoccupied corner.

"I got back as soon as I could," Harvey wheezed, his fist already wrapped around a mug of beer. He took a deep draw, then wiped his mouth on his sleeve.

Barrett crossed his arms, feeling just a bit uncharitable. "What happened to 'I'll be back in three hours'? It's afternoon, already."

The man offered a weak smile. "Major power failure. The whole East Coast went down for six minutes."

Barrett raised an eyebrow. "Only six? Then why are you so late? You know I could have used your help."

"It takes the time grid twelve hours to reboot and reestablish integrity. You wouldn't have me traveling through time by way of a faulty door, would you? Anyway, it sounds like you did just fine without me. Three people stopped me between the jail and here to tell me the story."

Barrett contemplated the moisture collecting on the outside of his mug. "It was close, Harvey. Too damn close. But I have a worse problem now."

"What?" Harvey took another gulp of his beer. "Damn, this stuff makes the beer of my day taste like water."

Irritation began to bead on Barrett's conscience. "Harvey, listen. This is important. I stopped Thornwald. He's in jail and won't be able to purchase any property from the townspeople."

Harvey slapped him on the back. "Well, congratulations, then. I'm just glad you put him in the second cell. If you hadn't, I'd have had to step over him when I emerged through the portal."

"Harvey . . ." Barrett paused to swallow hard. "Why haven't I returned to my own time?"

Suddenly, Earl loomed into view carrying a tray loaded with brimming glasses. Offered a fresh drink, Barrett indicated his half-full mug, but Harvey snagged two more beers, giving Barrett an apologetic look. "Hey . . . it's a long trip. I get thirsty!"

As soon as Earl wandered off, Barrett leaned closer to his companion. "Harvey, you've got to help me understand. Why haven't Johnny and I exchanged places?"

Harvey drained one beer. "I have absolutely no idea."

"A lot of help you are." Barrett released a sigh.

The time-traveler placed his empty mug on a nearby table. "Hey, don't forget, I'm the one who gave you the flashlight."

"Yeah . . ." Barrett shrugged. "I remember." He managed to find a smile from somewhere deep inside. "Go . . . go have fun. Maybe, when you come back, I'll be Johnny."

"S'long." Harvey ambled off, nursing the second beer.

Other people filled in the emptiness Harvey left behind, everyone wanting to hear the sheriff's version of the rescue. Halfway through the fifth discourse, Barrett saw Emma standing beyond the swinging saloon doors.

When she stepped through the entrance, he forgot he was in a room full of people. Rampant carnal thoughts danced the libido limbo in his mind. He was already in love with the brains, but viewing how she had been poured into a new dress, he realized that the body was fighting for equal recognition. And he wasn't the only one who noticed.

Conversations stopped in mid-word and the cacophony which had commanded the room suddenly dimmed. Emma collected every admiring male glance in the room. But it was Barrett who started the applause, with the townspeople quickly picking up the cue. The band started a rousing if not almost melodic version of "For He's a Jolly Good Fellow" which the partygoers sang in unschooled yet zealous voices with the appropriate gender change.

With a blush, Emma dropped her head, lifting it only momentarily to grace the room with an embarrassed smile. The crowd allowed Barrett to cut his way through to her and give her a hug, which started a whole new round of applause along with a few catcalls.

Before Emma could say anything, he gave her a wink and mouthed the words "Still me" as proof of his continuing identity. He lifted a hand to quiet the crowd.

"Ladies and gentlemen, I give you the true heroine of Margin, the woman . . ." He paused and grinned at her. "The doctor who risked her life to keep you all from being swindled out of your livelihoods and your properties." He held up his beer. "To Emma Nolan!"

"To Miss Nolan!"

"To Emma!"

"Three cheers!"

The crowd roared in unison three times, with their loud "Hip-hip hoorays" helping her turn from pale pink to bright red.

"Please . . ." she whispered to Barrett.

He leaned closer to her ear. "They put me through the same torture when I walked in."

"Speech! Speech!" the crowd echoed.

One voice could be heard above the rest. "Have you figured out why that scalawag wanted the mine so bad, Sheriff?"

Barrett shrugged. "There's copper there. Maybe that's what he wanted."

"And gold," Emma supplied.

The word spread throughout the room like wildfire. "Gold!"

Barrett gaped at her. "Where'd you get that idea? There's no gold in the Daisy Lee." He leaned closer and whispered so that only she could hear, "I certainly wouldn't be here if that mine had ever contained a speck of gold."

She shrugged. "I found the assayer's report Mr. Thornwald had performed on an ore sample from the mine. It said there was gold."

The voices of the crowd surged with excitement until a lone voice cut through the noise. "There ain't no gold."

"Oh yeah?" another voice challenged. "How you know?"

Lemuel the barber stood on a chair and waved his hands to silence the crowd. "I have a confession to make. When he first moved here, Mr. Thornwald came to me for a shave and mentioned how he had come West with dreams of owning a gold mine some day. And I knew the Daisy Lee weren't gonna last forever. So I took him on a little tour and suggested he take a sample from the 'Lucky Lady.'"

"You mean the Lady's really lucky?"

Lemuel ducked his head. "No, it means that's where my cousin and I salted the mine with some gold the night before. We figured Thornwald would get all het up and pay us big money for the land. Then the sheriff started talking about town loyalty and owning something that lasted to pass down to our kids . . ." The man shrank before their very eyes. "We felt bad, but there weren't nothin' we could do to stop Thornwald. He wouldn't believe we'd tricked him although we 'fessed up to it."

Earl began to laugh. "Would have served that scoundrel right if we *had* sold out to him! Gold!" His infectious laughter soon affected everybody in the place except the barber.

Lemuel raised his downcast gaze to look at Emma. "I'm so sorry, Miss Nolan. I never—"

She stopped him with a gesture. "Please, Mr. Thompkins, I can't say I would have approved of your deception, but I know you never meant for anyone to get hurt. And I'm sure everyone else feels that way."

He brightened perceptibly. "Thanks . . . Doc."

The last round of praise nearly deafened them, but after the cheers were over, the people returned to the time-consuming task of celebrating with food and drink.

Barrett led Emma through a gauntlet of admirers to an unoccupied table. People continued to speak to her for the next half hour, preventing them from conversing with each other. Finally, the newness of their heroics faded and they were left in relative peace.

"You look fantastic."

She graced him with a beautiful smile. "It was Penny's idea. She, Cara Brainard, and Jessie Soames decided I deserved a little pampering after the 'ordeal.' "

"They ought to go into the 'pampering' business. People in my day and time pay a fortune for such treatment." He reached across the table and took her hand, noticing how the long flowing sleeves of her blouse hid the bandages on both wrists. *Damn you, Thornwald* . . . "How are you doing . . . inside?"

She shrugged. "I'm all right." Her labored smile belied her simple words.

"It'll take awhile for the echoes, for the memories, to disappear. But he's in jail. He'll never be able to touch you again."

Her expression grew more at ease, and she squeezed Barrett's hand. "He didn't . . .

touch me. But thanks for worrying . . ." She squeezed again. "And caring."

And loving.

Whoa . . . where did that come from?

She continued, unaware of the momentous discovery he'd just made. "You know, I felt sure you'd be gone." She ducked her head and grinned. "I thought I'd have to explain it all to Johnny so he could play along and not sound like a complete fool."

"You may have to do that yet."

"Do you think it'll be instantaneous?"

"Maybe. I don't know." Suddenly, returning to his own time was the last thing on his mind. He stood, still holding her hand, and gently pulled her to her feet. "Let's not talk about that. Let's . . . dance!" *Maybe our first and last dance.*

The music and merriment provided the distraction he needed from his own thoughts while keeping him in relatively close proximity to Emma. He yearned for a song like "Unchained Melody," something which would get Emma tucked in his arms, but he had to settle for "After the Ball Is Over." To his utter surprise, he avoided her toes while sharpening his rusty waltz to match the caliber of the ragtag orchestra.

In the midst of the dance, someone tapped him on the shoulder. *No one's cutting in on this dance!* He turned and stared into Harvey's red-rimmed eyes. Although the man had obviously been drinking, there was a sober tone to his voice.

"Sheriff, I need to speak to you. Private." Harvey nodded toward the door.

Barrett turned to excuse himself, but Emma smiled. "Just don't be long."

"I promise. I'll take care of this and be right back."

Harvey hustled him out the swinging door and grabbed him by the arm, pulling him down the sidewalk.

Barrett extracted himself from the man's grasp. "I'd appreciate it if you'd tell me why you had to interrupt what might be my last dance with Emma."

"You'll understand in a minute."

Harvey led him back to the sheriff's office and flung open the door. *That's* our problem."

Barrett stepped into the room and scanned the shadows. He turned up the wick of the lamp on his desk and light flooded the dark corners of the office and cells. His prisoner in cell number one didn't react to the sudden glare.

Barrett pivoted to stare at his friend. "What's the problem, Harvey?"

"Him." The man pointed to Thornwald. "He's dead."

Barrett shoved his gun in Harvey's hand, jerked the keys out of his pocket, and unlocked the cell door. "Keep me covered." He crossed to the cot and squatted by the still form. A few moments later, he rocked back on his heels, feeling a knot the size of a soccer ball in the pit of his stomach.

Dead as the proverbial doornail.

"Maybe he had a heart attack, or something," Harvey offered.

"No . . ." Barrett stared at the dead man's face. "I don't think so. Wait . . . what's that?" He pointed to Thornwald's hair.

Harvey leaned over his shoulder and squinted at the body. "What's what?"

"That . . . white thing in his hair."

"I dunno." The man winced. "I'm not going to touch him and find out."

Barrett grimaced as he reached into the lock of hair which hung limply across Thornwald's forehead and plucked out the white object. Cradling it in the palm of his hand, he stared at it.

"It's a feather," Harvey stated in a slightly slurred voice.

"It's . . . down. Goose down."

"You mean like out of a ski parka?" Harvey's red-rimmed eyes grew larger. "You mean someone with a down-filled ski parka came in here and killed him? Someone from . . . the future!"

Barrett glared at Thornwald's body. Everything was too pat. The bandaged hands were crossed too precisely on his chest, the pillow unnaturally square in relation to the cot. Barrett studied Thornwald's lax face, then pointed to the man's forehead. "When I left him a couple of hours ago, his hair was parted on the other side."

Harvey gaped at Barrett. "You mean someone in a ski parka came in here, killed him, and combed his hair the wrong way?"

"Use your brain, Harvey! Someone from this time period took his pillow and smothered him in his sleep. Of course, he probably woke up and tried to fight off his attacker before he died. Look . . ." He pointed to the sloppy bandages. "Lemuel may be a lousy surgeon, but because of that he's had more than enough practice wrapping people in bandages. He didn't do anything that messy. Thornwald probably screwed them up when he fought back."

Harvey pounded him on the back. "This is fantastic!"

"What?" Barrett stood, suddenly catching the full brunt of Harvey's alcohol-scented breath. "Jeez, you stink. How many beers have you had?"

"Not too many. After all, I just figured out that your problems are over."

"What do you mean?"

"Up to now, there was always a chance, however slim, that Thornwald would beat the rap, and the people of Margin might still sell their land to him, or someone representing him."

"But—"

"But now they can't. He's dead. Stiff. Pushing up daisies. Sleeping with the fishes. There is now absolutely no way the people will sell to him." Harvey clapped him on the back. "It's been a gas, pal." He stepped back and crossed his arms as if he were waiting for Barrett to fade away.

Barrett, himself, half-expected the room to blur and be replaced by the executive washroom of Callan Industries. He held his breath.

Nothing happened.

"Nothing happened." He took a step toward Harvey.

"No . . . just give it a minute."

Barrett gave it a minute. Then two. Then five. "This is ridiculous. Nothing's going to happen."

Harvey swayed a bit. "Well . . . it's 'sposed to happen. I guess I could go forward and check to see if there's a reverse temporal wave holding back any changes."

"A reverse . . . what?"

"Temporal wave. It's a backflow problem. Changes occur in the past and their repercussions affect the future, but for some reason, the new future doesn't flow back down the chain to the past until someone crosses the temporal barrier and breaks the dam."

"Harvey . . . I have no idea what you're talking about."

"C'mere." Harvey gestured for Barrett to follow and led him to the second cell. Once inside, the man fumbled with his portal watch. "Let's shake the dam loose. See ya on the other side." Harvey disappeared through the stone wall.

Barrett suddenly saw Emma's face. "Wait, Harvey . . . Don't—"

Harvey stepped back into the room, scratching his head. "I don't understand." All signs of intoxication had faded from his face. "This isn't right."

"What?"

"I've never seen anything like this."

Barrett grabbed the man's vest. *"What?"*

"You've made bail. I mean, Johnny as Barrett made bail but it's just a matter of days before the sentencing."

Fear clutched Barrett's throat. "Sentencing?"

The man nodded. "Nothing's changed. Your company's gone down the tubes and Johnny's . . . er, your days of freedom are numbered."

"Then, Thornwald's death didn't change anything." Barrett's stomach tightened.

Harvey scratched his head again. "Or maybe his death has prevented the right changes from ever being made. If he wasn't supposed to die, then there may be a permanent temporal block."

"Meaning?"

"Neither you nor Johnny can return to your respective times. He's stuck there and you're stuck here."

"Forever?"

"Looks that way."

Barrett's hopes and dreams burned up right before his eyes, and from their ashes came a new hope and an even better dream.

Here . . . with Emma.

"Uh . . . you stay and . . . and watch him." Barrett thumbed back toward the late banker. "I've got something to do." He headed for the door.

"Hold it!" Harvey's voice broke. "Stay here? With him? You expect him to walk off when you turn your back?"

Barrett ignored the man and started down the sidewalk.

"You just remember what happened to your guest in here," Harvey called out from the office door. "And you make damn sure it doesn't happen to you."

Once Barrett reached the swinging doors of the Crystal Plume, he paused to tuck in his starched shirt and straighten his tie. Brushing off his vest, once Johnny's property, now his, Barrett drew a deep breath and walked into the room.

Emma sat at a table surrounded by, in his

opinion, way too many suitors. Most of them gave good-natured groans when they saw Barrett approach, and they said their quick farewells to her. Barrett glared at the remaining few, who quickly found excuses to leave in haste.

She gave him a guarded smile. "Are you always so unsociable at a party?"

He shrugged. "Sometimes. Can we talk?" He pulled out the chair next to hers.

"Everything all right?"

He looked into her eyes, hoping to find the answer to a question he hadn't even asked himself. What he saw in those blue depths gave him the courage to simply blurt out what he wanted to say.

"Emma . . . will you marry me?"

She stared at him, shock replacing the merriment which had filled her moments ago. "What?"

Barrett felt his face redden. "You aren't going to make me get down on one knee, are you?"

"Uh . . . no." She paled beneath her golden freckles.

"Is that 'No, I won't marry you' or 'No, I won't make you get on one knee'?"

"Um . . ." She made a fluttering gesture with her hand. "The bit about the knee."

"Good." He reached out and captured her hand. "Now, what about the other question?"

"But Johnny . . . you . . . the future!"

Barrett didn't want to spoil his proposal with the news of Thornwald's death, even if it was the incident which had stranded him in another time and place. "The future is whatever we want to make of it. I'm here to stay. And I can't imagine doing it without you. Now, your answer, please?"

She looked at him with more love than he'd ever seen before, far more than he'd ever deserve. Her whisper echoed like an explosion in his ears.

"Yes."

He knew the band was playing, that people were shouting to be heard above the racket, that the world revolved around the sun and the sun spun in space, but all he cared about was Emma. He leaned forward and their lips met in the sweetest, most tender kiss that any man had ever experienced in the chronicles of all time and history. He could have stayed there forever if the outside world hadn't penetrated his consciousness with its sudden silence.

The band had stopped playing. The people were quiet. The couple broke apart only to find they were the center of attention in the bar.

A cheer rose from the "ladies" watching from the balcony, and the people below echoed the sentiment. Emma covered her blushing face with her hands and Barrett wished he could do the same. But instead, he stood.

"You better explain yourself, Sheriff," called out Earl from the bar. The crowd laughed.

"I'm not accustomed to making speeches, but it looks like I have another announcement to make. I'm pleased to say Miss Emma Nolan, a very brave, very smart, and very beautiful doctor, has agreed to be my wife."

The pandemonium resumed, and Barrett and Emma again became the center of attraction in the room. Ford battled his way through the crowd to give his sister a hug and solemnly shake his impending brother-in-law's hand. Earl broke into his very special champagne stock and the town leaders took turns toasting the couple-to-be.

In the middle of the celebration, Barrett glanced up and saw Jimmie Soames standing in the doorway. The deputy gestured to him. It wasn't as much the urgency of the gesture as the look on Jimmie's face which made Barrett excuse himself and head out.

"Jimmie, what's wrong?"

"We got a problem, Sheriff. A big problem." The young man fidgeted with his gun belt.

"What is—"

Jimmie grabbed his arm. "Let's talk outside."

As soon as they exited the noisy building,

Barrett stopped the deputy. "Listen, if it's about Thornwald, I already know he's dead. Harvey and I found him."

Jimmie paled, then grabbed him by the arm. "I've got to show you something."

When they stepped into the office, Barrett reached to turn up the lamp, but Jimmie stopped him.

"Don't. I don't want anyone to know we're in here."

"So, what's going on?"

"Bank's gonna be robbed."

Barrett felt a prickle dance up his spine. "When?"

"Tonight."

"Did you overhear something?"

Jimmie's hand snaked down to his gun butt. "I overheard you and Thornwald talking about it. He gave you his keys and told you the safe combination."

Barrett gaped at the young man. "You've got to be crazy . . ." He looked into his deputy's gun barrel and inspiration hit, a moment too late. "Or desperate." He hesitated for a second, then spoke softly. "It was you, wasn't it?"

Although visibly nervous, Jimmie kept his trigger finger stock still.

Barrett continued. "You're the one who smothered Thornwald. No one else had the keys to the cell but you and me. What, were you afraid he'd spill the beans and tell me how you helped him concoct his scheme? He needed an inside man, a local who could help him set up the people." He searched his deputy's face for some sign of regret. "Why? Why, Jimmie?"

Soames stiffened. "I have children who need more than I can provide right now. This job doesn't pay enough and unlike most of the folks around here, I don't own any land. So all the fancy talk about leaving a legacy to the next generation is nothing but bunkum to me."

"But . . ." Barrett stared into the dimly lit cells, realizing there were two bodies, one in the bed and the other sprawled on the floor. *Harvey!* Barrett stepped toward the deputy. "I don't—"

"Shut up, Johnny. We're going to the bank. If you say anything, do anything, by God, I'll shoot you." Jimmie draped his coat over his arm, concealing the gun. "Go."

The only noise which littered the town strayed from the Crystal Plume. Otherwise, the streets were desolate. Jimmie had them walk on the opposite side of the street, away from the saloon.

Barrett paused directly across from the saloon. "So I'm supposed to rob the bank and disappear with the money?"

"Something like that. Keep on going."

"No."

The simple defiance seemed to take the

deputy by surprise. Then the man's face blanched as a group of people spilled out of the saloon doors.

"There he is! Johnny, wait a minute. Here he is, Miss Emma."

Emma, no!

Emma stepped off the porch and quickly crossed the street. "Is anything wrong?"

Barrett spoke first, hoping to get her away from danger. "No problem. Jimmie and I have a bit of business to conduct, then I'll be right back."

She smiled. "All right. I just—" She stopped, then pointed down the street. "Isn't that Mr. Kirk?"

The next few moments demonstrated just how alternately cruel and kind the element of time had been to Barrett. It took only a split second for Harvey to stumble out of the office and sag against the hitching post, pointing an accusing finger at Jimmie Soames.

It took eons for Barrett to get to Emma, spin her around, and push her back toward the saloon. Caught in his deceptions like a scared rabbit in a trap, Jimmie panicked and swung the gun up, aiming at Barrett.

As the gun fired, Barrett looked into the terrified eyes of the woman he loved. Just beyond her, Ford appeared on the saloon porch, his scream blending with the percussion which filled Barrett's ears.

Absolute blackness blanketed him, blotting out his view of Emma. Something warm and sticky flowed on his hands, and the sound of screams replaced the echoes of the gun.

"She's dead! You let her die! You let my sister die!"

Barrett's world began to spin, and Ford's screams spun with it.

"Why couldn't it be you?

Why couldn't it be you?

Why couldn't it be . . ."

Fourteen

As Emma regained her senses, she could hear Ford's screams, but she centered her awakening attention on the unconscious man lying on top of her. She pushed away the hands which tried to guide her away from her medical duties.

She was the doctor. *She* would attend to her beloved's wounds.

They carried Barrett's body into the Crystal Plume and she hovered over him, searching for the bullet wound to treat. "Help me roll him over," she commanded to the gaping crowd. "He must have gotten it in the back."

Penny pushed her way through the crowd. "If you're not going to help Emma, then get out of our way!" she yelled to the shocked bystanders.

With Penny's strong help, Emma examined Barrett thoroughly, but found no wound other than a lump on the back of his head. Penny patted her on the shoulder. "Child, he's just taken a blow to the noggin. He'll be fine when he wakes up. Silas, Earl . . . get some of the boys to help carry the sheriff up to his room."

Emma began to shake. "But I saw the blood. I saw his expression when the bullet hit him. I know he was shot." Someone helped her into a chair and shoved a drink in her hands. "He was trying to protect me. Shield me . . ." Emma remembered Ford's screams. She tried to stand but her legs wouldn't support her. "Where's my brother? Where's Ford?"

Cara Brainard brought the sobbing boy to Emma. When he saw his sister, he threw himself in her lap.

"I saw the deputy . . . and then the sheriff." He gulped for breath between sobs. "And when the gun w-went off, I thought he was trying to hide . . . to hide b-behind y-you . . . and I s-saw the blood and thought . . . I thought . . ." He buried his head in her shoulder and uncontrolled convulsions racked his small body. She pulled him completely into her lap, soothing him with whispers and a tight grasp. After a minute, he lifted his swollen face from her wet shoulder.

"Is he . . . is Johnny going to be all right?"

"Yes, Ford. He'll be fine. He'll just have a headache when he wakes."

Emma dabbed away her own tears and took Ford resolutely by the hand. Brushing off the help of the townspeople, she marched out of the saloon and headed for the boarding house. Penny was sitting by Barrett's bed, and she smiled when Emma appeared in the doorway.

"I knew you wouldn't be far behind me, Emma. You're made of strong stuff, girl."

"Thanks, Penny. I left Ford downstairs in the kitchen. I . . . I don't think he ought to be alone."

The big woman smiled and rose from the chair. "I understand. I think I can find some gingerbread down there and keep the two of us occupied." She paused in the door to give Emma an enveloping hug. "I think he's about to wake, and it's your face he needs to see first."

Emma took Penny's station by the bed, watching her husband-to-be fight his way out of his unconsciousness. Finally, he threw an arm over his eyes and groaned.

"Barrett? Wake up. Everything's fine."

He responded to her voice and seemed just on the edge of waking up.

"Barrett, you're all right. You're safe."

He opened his eyes and looked at her and she knew instinctively who he was.

Johnny Callaghan.

The echoes died away as Barrett's world refracted into a million pieces. When they

reassembled, the spinning blackness lightened until everything was bright white.

And cold.

Heaven, hell, or Johnny's limbo?

He pushed himself to his feet after discov-
ering he still had a pair of them attached to
his ankles. The noises around him didn't
sound like souls being tortured, nor angels
playing their harps. Raising a hand to his
face, he found he had some sort of goggles
protecting his eyes. Brushing his fingers
across the lenses removed the filmy layer of
white and revealed exactly where he was.

In snow.

Barrett twisted around to scan his location,
this new reality.

Skiers barreled past him, some hellbent
for leather, others making gentle, sweeping
curves through the snow.

A ski slope?

He glanced at his hand, ignoring the pole
which dangled from his wrist by a strap. It
was the sleeve of his outfit which caught his
attention. It was neon orange and green,
piped in black, and was the most God-awful
thing Barrett had ever seen in his life.

He sucked in a gulp of the cold air, hoping to clear a mind which was evidently hal-
lucinating. Where was Emma? He looked
around, belatedly remembering the final moments before awakening face-first in the
snow.

Oh God . . . I've got to get to Emma. I've got to get to—

Barrett stared at the skis clipped to the awkward boots encasing his feet. Gravity started to inch him down the slope toward the mountain lodge at the base. As he reached to brace himself with the poles, a searing pain attacked his left shoulder, radiating down his arm and into his chest.

"Emma," he grunted against the pain. "Gotta get to Emma."

He pushed off, clutching his left arm to the front of his garish ski jacket.

Then the dilemma of the situation hit him like a ton of snow.

"But I don't know how to s-k-i-i-i . . ."

The scenery pitched and rotated as he tumbled down the slope. The skis detached early on, leaving just him to cartwheel in front of other skiers, testing their avoidance abilities.

When he grew cognizant of a world which had stopped spinning, he realized he lay on his back in the snow, staring into a cloudless sky. Concerned faces pushed into his view.

"Don't worry, sir. We're the Ski Patrol and we've handled . . ." The calm face paled. "Oh shit! Mr. Callaghan!" The young man nearly dropped his radio. "Patrol One to Base. The Eagle has landed . . . I mean, the Eagle has fallen. Priority Code Two."

Another face loomed into view. "Mr. Callaghan, can you tell me where it hurts?"

"M-my shoulder." Barrett raised his right hand to indicate the place and realized he'd lost a glove in the process of falling. He managed to slip his fingers in the open front of his jacket, but when he removed them, they were coated with blood.

Gentle but firm hands took over, unzipping his jacket and revealing the bloody wound. One man slapped a bandage over the hole and barked at the other. "Upgrade it to a Priority Code One Red. Now!"

The younger man blanched completely but repeated the orders into the radio.

The man leaned over Barrett, holding pressure to his shoulder. "Now, call in a Disaster Code Alpha."

"A what?"

"You heard me. Do it."

The second one stuttered over the words but managed to convey the message. He turned to the older one. "But what happened? Isn't it just a puncture wound from a tree branch or something like that?"

"Hell no, it isn't. Someone shot the boss."

Somewhere in the back of his mind Barrett heard the claxxons sounding, but the noise blended in with the sirens and the chop of helicopter blades. He tried to surrender to the more peaceful sensation of settling into the white clouds and letting his body rest, but the people around him refused to let him relax. They kept screaming orders and sticking things in him.

In the midst of the rescue, he looked into the nearest face and tried to make the too-serious young man smile. "This is a helluva way for me to experience my first helicopter ride."

The young man almost panicked, hastily checking the bottles strung across and the lines feeding intravenous drips into Barrett. Another medic began to play flashlight games with Barrett's eyes and whisper serious things to his younger cohort. "How much farther to Nolan General?"

"Almost there." The man turned to Barrett. "Don't worry, Mr. Callaghan. Everything'll be all right." The young medic turned to his companion. "He must really be out of it. He flies this rig more often than his pilot does."

He tried to correct the young man, but fatigue commanded oblivion and Barrett surrendered.

He woke up a few times, on each occasion finding himself somewhere different. The first time was in an elevator just as the doors opened. People rushed around him, pushing his gurney down a long hall at a fast trot. He counted the lights in the ceiling as they whizzed by.

"Sniper victim, Room One."

Sniper? Jimmie Soames wasn't a sniper. He might have been a fool, but he was no sniper.

When he awoke again, he tried to tell the doctors the very important piece of information about Jimmie, but they ignored him, instead cutting through the ugly ski suit and pausing to gape over the healed gunshot wound which Emma had so painstakingly treated.

The third time he awoke he was in a dark room, quiet except for an occasional snuffle from somewhere near the foot of the bed. As his eyes grew more accustomed to the dimness, he recognized the figure slumped in a chair across the room.

"Angela?"

Her head sprang up, and she nearly knocked the chair over in her efforts to get to him.

"Oh darling, you're awake! I was so worried."

His secretary lowered the rail and leaned over him. Her fragrance had intoxicated him for years. Her figure had tantalized him with its delicious "look but don't touch" curves. Her face had fueled many a dream and fantasy which ranked him at the top of the list of The Most Sexually Frustrated Men in America.

It was the same perfume, the same figure and face, but now it didn't matter.

Angela pressed her mouth against his,

performing a very adequate imitation of the kiss of life, but his heart didn't stir. His hormones didn't even budge. He felt absolutely nothing. All his dreams and fantasies of a past life had come true, but now it meant nothing to him.

When she pulled back from him, confusion marred her lovely features. Then the consternation cleared and sadness took its place.

"You're not Johnny."

They certainly weren't the words he expected to hear, but it saved a lot of needless explanation. "No. It's me. Barrett."

Angela sighed, her beauty suddenly becoming less a matter of cosmetics and more a part of the inner woman. "We knew this could happen. But we couldn't fight it."

"Fight what?"

"Attraction. Love."

"You and Johnny?"

She produced a sad smile and held up her hand, displaying a sizable chunk of diamond. "We're engaged." She sat on the edge of the bed, unable to hide her sadness. "At least, we were. Now I'm engaged . . . to you."

"Listen, Angela. I wouldn't make you . . . I mean I like you, but I wouldn't . . ." He drew a deep breath. "Angela, I fell in love with you the first moment I met you, and I did everything I could think of to make you love me. But . . ."

"But now you love someone else," she supplied.

Barrett nodded.

Her face softened. "Someone from Johnny's world?"

He nodded again, this time because his own emotions prevented him from speaking. Had Emma survived the gunplay? Did Johnny step back into his own world and take up the life Barrett had abandoned?

But there would be no answers outside of a history book. It was over a hundred years ago. Everyone was dead.

He struggled to change the topic. "Everything's changed." He stared into Angela's brown eyes, noticing the welling tears. "What was I doing on a ski slope? I don't know how to ski."

She sniffled into a tissue. "Of course you do. You own that ski slope. You own all of Margin Mountain Resort."

"M-Margin Mountain . . ."

"You know. Vail, Aspen, and Margin. The three biggest ski areas in Colorado."

Shock made the room spin. "I own a ski resort? But what about the mining operation?"

"Johnny . . ." She paused to wipe her eyes. "Johnny said there'd be some gaps in your memory, but I didn't think it would be this bad." She patted his uninjured arm. "This used to be a mining area back some time ago, but I don't think your family had anything to do with the mining operations. Callaghan Resorts has been the name of the business since your grandfather started things fifty years ago."

A ski resort . . . and the name . . . Callaghan. Apparently, no one had felt the need to change the name to "Callan." Strangely enough, he didn't mind losing one name and gaining the other. He'd gotten used to "Callaghan" in Margin.

"Where am I now? Denver?"

She shook her head. "There was no need to fly you there. Nolan General has always been a fine hospital. You've always said so . . ." She stopped. "At least, I think it was you. It might have been . . . Johnny." A new cascade of tears poured down her face.

Nolan . . . Emma's hospital. Had she survived to become a doctor in Margin, or had the hospital been named as a memorial to a dead woman who had hoped to become a physician one day?

"Angela . . ." He reached up and awkwardly patted her hand. "We're both in the same boat. And if I thought crying would help, I'd bawl right along with you. I . . . I had just gotten engaged myself before I returned." He stared at the rock resting on

Angela's left hand. "I wish I could have bought Emma a stone like that. I don't even know whether she survived or was shot when I was."

Angela stared at him, then slowly nodded. "So that's how you got shot without getting a hole in your ski suit. Now it makes sense! But how are you going to explain it to the police? They've been questioning all sorts of people, trying to find a witness. It's caused havoc at the resort because we thought there was a sniper out there."

"No, the sniper was a corrupt deputy named Soames who lived a hundred years ago."

A soft knock echoed through the room and a doctor stood silhouetted in the doorway. "I'm afraid you'll have to wait outside, miss." He stepped inside and the door swung closed.

Angela leaned over, pulled up the bed rail, and placed a chaste kiss on Barrett's forehead. "We'll talk later . . . boss. Try to get some rest."

Barrett closed his eyes and tried to formulate a plan to explain his ignorance of the new world he found himself thrust into.

"Now that's what I call a good-lookin' dame! After seeing her, I see why you wanted to get back here so bad."

"Harvey!"

The man had on a white lab coat and held

a metal clipboard in one hand. He gave Barrett a toothy grin. "C'est moi!"

"What are you doing . . . how did you . . ." Barrett grabbed the bed rails and tried to pull himself up. "Is Emma all right?"

"Whoa, buddy! You just lie back and let Dr. Kirk review the situation. First of all, yes, she's fine. Soames only fired one shot and you took the bullet with you into the future. I bet the police lab boys here are going to be pulling their hair out over this one. Can you imagine the ballistics crew telling their chief you were shot with a hundred-year-old bullet?"

"I thought I was stuck in the past. Why all of the sudden did I come back?"

"Now that was a hard one." Kirk pulled a chair around the end of the bed and plopped down. "I had to do a little research up and down the line to figure that out."

"Well?"

"It seems that Thornwald wasn't the temporal pivot in your problems."

"Temporal pivot?"

"The thing which needed to change in order to give you a new future. I found out that—"

They both heard a knock on the door. The figure stepped into the room, hidden by the shadows.

"Doc, I promise I'll only stay a minute."

Crawford James!

Anger boiled up in Barrett and he wanted to wrap his hands around the embezzler's throat. "Crawford, you—"

The man gave him a genuinely warm smile. "Hey, boss. How ya feeling? Angela said you were awake. Listen, I just wanted to let you know everything's being handled. We're already getting some good press about our people's efficiency in evacuating the slopes. We've issued lift passes for all the daytimers and a free night's lodging for the overnighters. Everything'll be fine."

"In no *time* at all," Harvey supplied with a wink, motioning for Barrett to be quiet. "I'm afraid you'll have to leave, Mr. James. Perhaps Mr. Callaghan will feel up to company later on."

Barrett stared at Harvey, then at the man who he thought had swindled his company out of a cool couple of million. "But . . ."

"Doctor's orders. Later."

Crawford James waved and ducked out the door.

Barrett pointed toward the closing door. "I thought . . ."

Harvey shook his head. "That was the old history. In this new version, that's Crawford James, your very trusted vice president. He's not an embezzler. In fact, Crawford James is none other than Emma Nolan's great-grand-nephew."

"Emma's?"

"Yep . . . Crawford James was named after his great-grandfather, Crawford Nolan. Only you and I knew him as 'Ford.' You see, according to my recollection, you saved Emma's life three times. Once at the saloon, where it turns out that bullet that hit you was supposed to have killed her by accident. The second was at the mine. Apparently she was fated to die in a cave-in. And the third happened when Jimmie Soames shot you; again, it was meant for her."

Barrett felt his shoulder fire up again. Was the medication wearing off, or was it the pain of reliving the shooting?

Harvey continued. "In the original scenario, Ford witnessed his sister's death and blamed it on Johnny. In fact, the boy became quite insistent that Johnny had used Emma as a shield and allowed her to die in his place."

"But Johnny wouldn't do something like that," Barrett argued.

"I know that. In fact everyone knew that, even Johnny. But a great loss can have quite an effect on a person, and it turned Ford Nolan from a bright boy with a future to a scheming young man with a mission."

"A mission?"

"It took four more generations to accomplish the deed. It was like the Hatfields and the McCoys, but the McCoys didn't know there was a war going on. No one seemed to realize that when something went unexpectedly wrong with the Callaghan clan, there was always a Nolan nearby who was to blame. Remember when your father's plane exploded?"

Barrett nodded, recalling his father's near miss back in the seventies.

"Well, the pilot was Crawford James's uncle, a Nolan."

"But now . . . in this new history, Emma didn't die."

Harvey leaned back in his chair and smiled. "Exactly, and the whole vendetta thing never occurred. Crawford James is exactly what he appears to be, a bright young man with a great future in the ski resort industry. He's no criminal. None of the Nolans have been criminals."

"What about Emma?" Barrett expected to hear the crash when his heart dropped and shattered into a thousand pieces. "I guess she married Johnny."

Harvey shrugged. "Not necessarily. In fact, she never married. She went back to school in Michigan, got her medical degree, and set up practice in Margin. Johnny married your great-great-grandmother, and the rest, as they say, is history."

"Emma never married before she died? Why?"

"Who knows? Maybe she never found the

right man." Harvey gave him a raised-eye-brow stare. "Or maybe she couldn't have the man she really loved."

Barrett pushed back in his pillow, bemoaning what must have been a life full of dedication and work for Emma without the counterbalance of love and devotion. Maybe she was a woman born to be a doctor, but she was a woman born to be cherished as well. A woman he wanted to cherish every day of her life.

Change the subject, he commanded himself. *Say anything, but change the subject.* "What about the mine?"

Harvey nodded his head slightly, as if he understood Barrett's self-preservation tactics. "I didn't research that far. All I know is because Thornwald died, Johnny didn't become a partner in the mining business. I have no idea how your family got wrapped up in the ski industry."

"And all this time I thought keeping the townspeople consolidated against Thornwald would be the spark which might change everything. I guess Johnny thought that, too."

Harvey shifted uncomfortably in his chair. "I wouldn't be so sure of that."

Barrett stared at the time-traveler. "You think Johnny knew the truth? That everything went wrong because Ford witnessed Emma's death?"

"I do." Harvey fiddled with the stethoscope hanging around his neck. "I really do. But we could find out for sure—that is, if you wanted to."

Barrett gripped the bed rails again, wondering if he understood why Harvey was smiling. "Find out? How?"

The time-traveler pulled the portal watch out of his coat pocket and dangled it in front of Barrett.

"We can ask Johnny ourselves."

Fifteen

Johnny stepped out of the house and onto the porch where Emma sat in the rocking chair. "Emma, you still want those shelves hung between the windows?"

"Yes, please." She tried with near desperation to give him a smile, but it wouldn't stick to her face. "I appreciate how you're spending your day off to help me construct this new dispensary."

He nodded. "Don't mind the work. Whole town'll benefit from it."

"I'll come in and help—"

He waved her back to her chair. "No, ma'am. You've worked hard enough today. Just sit there, enjoy the sunset, and I'll be through in a short while."

After he turned and went back into the house, Emma couldn't prevent one of her silent tears from escaping and rolling down her cheek.

He looked so much like Barrett, sometimes even acted like Barrett. But this Johnny Callaghan, as good a man as he certainly was, couldn't replace Barrett Callan in life.

In her memories.

In her heart.

Emma was in love with, pining over, a man who hadn't even been born yet. She'd be dead and buried for many years before he even drew his first breath of air.

It's unfair, she sobbed to herself. *It's so totally unfair!* Faced with such internal devastation, she found the brilliant orange sunset to be strangely unsatisfying. It merely served to mark one more long day on earth without Barrett. She leaned forward, covered her face with her hands, and allowed her sobs to surface and bubble out.

After a few minutes, the part of her which professed to be strong began to chide Emma for her overwhelming weaknesses. Responsibility, duty, the common good . . . these would have to replace love and devotion in her world, in her heart. She dried her eyes with her ever-present handkerchief, stood, and paused in the doorway of her house-cum-dispensary, trying to find some strains of beauty in the sunset.

"Emma . . ."

The voice came from a distance.

Perhaps from her imagination.

"Emma!"

The second echo was stronger.

She scanned the street, spotting two men

walking toward her house, one leaning heavily on the other. She sighed, realizing that, although the dispensary might not be finished, it appeared it would be christened with a new patient.

Emma called through the open door. "Johnny? I think we may have a patient coming." She glanced into the street again, this time viewing an apparition . . .

A specter.

An impossibility.

Her heart caught in her throat, wedging out the ability to breathe.

Barrett . . .

She stumbled down the stairs and stopped in shock at the sight. She whispered his name over and over, as if the hushed words would guarantee she wasn't dreaming.

Harvey Kirk was part of the hallucination. He was half-supporting, half-dragging her beloved Barrett Callan down the street.

She looked down at their feet, seeing the long shadows which streamed across the ground. They were real. Unable to release the stair rail for fear she'd fall, Emma twisted her head toward the door. "Johnny? Johnny? Oh Good Lord . . . hurry!"

The sheriff of Margin appeared in the doorway, wiping his hands on a towel. "What's wrong? I could hear—" He stopped in mid-word as he turned his unconcerned gaze toward the street. When he recognized the two approaching men, Johnny vaulted into action, jumping the porch rail, racing to his great-great-grandson's side.

The moment Johnny touched Barrett, something broke loose in Emma. She pulled her grip loose from the wooden rail and ran toward the man she loved. "Oh Barrett! You . . . you came back."

His kiss erased every moment of sadness and pain she'd experienced in her entire life, eradicating any thoughts of abandonment and loneliness. He whispered wonderful things in her ear, ran his hands over her face with alternate gentleness and ferocity.

Tears and laughter mixed as she pulled back and gave him a complete once-over. "Is this what they wear in the twentieth century?" She eyed his loose-fitting faded green pants and shirt. Black initials had been painted above the pocket: *NMH*. Harvey wore something similar in white, with the same three letters.

"No, it's only what well-respected and well paid physicians wear in the twentieth century."

"And twenty-second century, too." Harvey Kirk had a tight hold on Barrett, as if he were instrumental to holding her beloved upright.

Barrett stared at Harvey. "Wait, you mean you're not from my time?"

The man grinned back. "So how many

twentieth-century time machines have you ever seen outside of TV or the movies, buddy-boy?" Barrett continued to stare gape-mouthed at Harvey, who winked at Emma. "I'm sorry, ma'am. I had to pump him full of painkillers to make sure he made it through the portal."

"Painkillers? Portals?" Emma glared at Harvey, then at Barrett, then at Johnny. "Johnny, can *you* explain any of this to me?"

"Just as soon as we get the boy into your new dispensary. I think he's sprung a leak." Johnny moved his hand back, revealing a growing spot of blood on Barrett's shoulder.

"Good Lord, I was right. You *were* shot!" The efficient doctor in Emma came to the surface. "Carry him inside before anybody sees him. And for heaven's sake, be careful with his shoulder!"

Harvey and Johnny half-carried, half-dragged an uncooperative Barrett into the dispensary and placed him on the examination table.

"But I keep telling you, I feel fine." He tried to bat away their hands, but when Emma stepped closer he made no efforts to hinder her inspection of his wound.

The medical care he'd received exceeded anything she'd ever seen before. The knotted stitches that closed the wound were tiny, precise, and made of a material she'd never encountered. His bleeding had come from one stitch that had torn open. Otherwise, she anticipated his full recovery from his injury with minimal scarring.

When she proclaimed her patient none the worse for wear, Johnny and Harvey cheered. Barrett merely used his good arm to pull her into an embarrassing, decadent, and thoroughly enjoyable kiss.

Once they broke apart, Barrett gave Johnny a wide grin. "Well, Great-Great-Grandaddy, I appreciate you watching over my girl, but I think there's someone who's pining for you back in the twentieth century."

Johnny crossed his arms. "I wish it was that simple, boy. But I belong here and you belong there."

Barrett shook his head. "Explain it to him, Harvey."

Harvey held out his watch. "You and I can go through the portal together, Johnny. I'll drop you off in the twentieth century on my way through."

"But I don't belong there."

Barrett smiled at his great-great-grandfather. "Ah, but you do. You have a wonderful woman waiting for you and a great business, plus, I understand you're a fantastic skier. As for myself, I can't stand the sport. Can you imagine a non-skier owning one of the largest resorts in Colorado?"

"But I—"

Emma raised her hand to stop Johnny. She turned to Harvey. "I assume you've been hiding your true talents all the while. Are you indeed a time-traveler?"

Harvey nodded.

"And you can take Johnny to the future? And leave Barrett here with me?"

He nodded again.

She turned to Johnny. "Do you want to go?"

After a second of hesitation, he smiled. "Yes . . . yes, I do."

She turned to Barrett, again astounded at the physical similarities between the men. "Do you want to stay?"

He gave her an eerie smile reminiscent of Johnny's. "Absolutely."

She turned to Harvey. "Then I don't see what the problem is."

The man began to laugh, then reached up to give her a quick hug. "That's what I like about this woman. She cuts through all the nonsense about temporal distortion, genetic shock waves, and trickle-down transitory displacement. Gentlemen, let's put it this way. I won't tell if you don't." He turned to Johnny. "Uh, why don't you take Emma to the kitchen to say your goodbyes. There're a few details I have to go over with Barrett before we leave."

Johnny ushered her out of the dispensary and into the kitchen. "Sit down. I'll get us

some coffee." He poured two mugs and sat
down beside her, handing her one. He contemplated his cup. "You know . . . they have
flavored coffees in the future. And they put
some sort of artificial milk in it instead of
the real stuff." He took a long sip of the
brew then leaned back and closed his eyes.
"But Barrett's secretary, Angela, she learned
how to make it just right for me. Strong,
hot, and black."

"This Angela . . . is she why you're returning?"

A flush crept over his face and he cracked
open one eye. "You don't miss much, do
you?" He shifted toward her and stared into
his coffee cup. "Yep, Angela's why I'm going
back. She's . . . she's something different,
something very special. And I think Barrett
must think the same about you. It's not every
man who'll get out of a hospital bed and go
back in time a hundred years to see the
woman he loves."

"I don't understand how all of this started
or why it's ended the way it has. And I'm
not so sure those two in there have many
more answers than we do."

"Maybe we don't need answers. Maybe all
we need is faith."

"Faith," Emma repeated. "I like that.
Faith that it'll all work out."

He nodded. "Faith that we'll take the right
type of advantage from this unusual chance

to change our lives. Can I tell you a secret, Emma?"

"What?"

He leaned forward in conspiracy. "You're going to make a helluva doctor."

"A real one?"

He ran a finger along his jaw and grinned. "That's for me to know and for you to find out."

Barrett managed to sit up without feeling the room spin. "I didn't know there was a second set of rules to follow when you're breaking the first set."

"There isn't. I just wanted this time to give you one last choice."

Barrett shook a finger at the man. "Oh, no. My mind's made up. I'm staying here with Emma. I thought that was already established."

"No, it's not that." Harvey grew unnaturally solemn. "I want to warn you about your memory."

"My memory? Oh . . . I get it! This is the part where you tell me you're really an alien historian slash scientist from another planet and you can mind-meld with me and help me to forget . . ." Barrett did his best imitation of Spock.

Harvey shook his head. "Actually, I'm not

even an historian. At least not a professional
one. I'm really a plumber."

"A what?" Barrett bellowed.

"Sshh . . . they'll hear you." Harvey indicated the door. "I said I'm a plumber, which
is a very well-respected profession in the
twenty-second century."

"And your world lets plumbers hop a-
round in time machines and screw around
with history?"

Harvey appeared injured by Barrett's atti-
tude. "I'm not screwing around. It was an
uncontrollable cross-temporal event which
happened through no intercession of my
own."

"You even sound Vulcan."

"It means it was an accident that you and
Johnny met and it's not my fault. The Pow-
ers That Be believe the best way to clean up
the leakage from one century to the next is
to let you two choose where you want to stay.
Then the portal will be sealed after you
make your decision."

"How does this affect my memory?"

Harvey released his breath in a long
whoosh. "This gets difficult. Remember how
I had to spend Saturday nights in the portal
or risk forgetting all about myself, including
how to get back to my proper time?"

"I remember . . . go on."

"That's going to happen to you once the
portal closes. And I thought you ought to

know that before you made your final choice."

"I'll forget? Just like that?"

"No. It'll be gradual. A little bit each day. And it won't affect your life here in the past. In fact, it'll make it easier. You won't spend time wishing you have a microwave or a jet plane or something you know exists in the future but doesn't here. You'll eventually become Sheriff Johnny Callaghan and not remember your life as Barrett Callan."

"What about Emma?"

"Her memories are set. She'll know everything about how you got here. The removal of the time door won't affect her. Only you."

"But I won't forget Emma, will I?"

"Good God no. You won't forget anybody who's a part of your life here. Just those in the future, because they wouldn't have existed yet."

"Well . . . it's not a hard decision. I stay. With Emma. Just one more question, though. How come I didn't forget anything while I *was* here? Doesn't that blow your theory?"

The man's face split in a big grin. "No, you have your good friend Harvey Kirk to thank for that." He reached into his pocket and pulled out a sheriff's badge. "It's a miniaturized remote stabilizer. When I realized what Johnny had planned, I knew you'd never last without some external help to keep your memory boosted."

Barrett took the star from Harvey and examined it cautiously. "I never knew . . ."

"And you would never have remembered anything without it."

They both heard a knock on the door. Johnny's voice echoed from the hallway, sounding eerily like Barrett. "You two through in there?"

Barrett glanced at his friend. "Are we?"

Harvey nodded. "Afraid so. I've got to get back, but let me tell you . . . it's been a hell of a vacation. If I ever again save up enough money for a time share, I'll look you up." His face reddened. "That is, if they haven't revoked my passport." He stuck out his hand. "Friends?"

Barrett pulled the man into an awkward hug. "I'll never forget you, Harvey."

The man laughed. "You say that now . . ." He turned to the door. "We're through, Johnny."

Barrett's twin walked through the door and smiled at him. "Couple of questions."

"Shoot."

"How come you and Angela never developed a relationship?"

"Probably for the same reason you and Emma never hooked up." Barrett sighed. "Not the right time, the right place, or the right person."

Johnny nodded thoughtfully. "Second question: how can you have lived your whole life in Colorado and never learned to ski?"

Barrett shrugged. "Just lucky, I guess."

Emma appeared in the doorway. "Harvey says it's time to go." Barrett felt a sudden stab of jealousy when she reached up and hugged his doppelgänger. "Take care of yourself, Johnny. And your lady, too."

Barrett slipped off the table and found he could stand unsupported. "Johnny?" He held out his hand and his great-great-grandfather shook it with gentle resolution.

"Take care . . . boy. Remember, you've got a reputation to maintain. Mine!"

"And you just remember that life is more than moguls and ski bunnies."

Barrett slipped an arm around Emma and together they followed Harvey and Johnny to the porch.

"Don't come out," cautioned Johnny. "If anyone sees two Sheriff Callaghans, you'll have a bit of fancy stepping to do. And I don't think you're quite up to it yet, boy."

Barrett gestured with one hand. "I've crossed a century, landed into a strange life, and lived to tell about it. Twice. Explaining two Johnnys would be a piece of cake."

After the men left, Barrett turned to Emma, wishing he could put both arms around her. "You are the most beautiful, the smartest, the sweetest woman in the world."

She placed a hand on his forehead. "And you, sir, are a snake oil salesman who's on his way to becoming delirious. Those doctors in the future . . . don't they know anything about gunshot wounds?" She tucked her arm back around his waist. "C'mon, you. Back to the dispensary. You're going to be my first official patient."

With uncooperative muscles growing heavier moment by moment, Barrett managed to walk with Emma's help back to the dispensary bed. His energy gave out seconds after he laid his head on the pillow. The room grew darker and her smile sweeter.

"Just remember one thing."

She brushed the hair from his forehead with cool, gentle fingers. "What, sweetheart?"

He fought the growing darkness.

"Buy . . ."

"What, Barrett? I can't understand you. Say it again."

"Buy I.B.M."

Epilogue

From the journal of John B. Callaghan
January 1, 1900

The morning sunrise heralds the dawn of not only a new day, but a new century. As I look back over the entries of previous years, I still find it hard to believe that this is not my rightful place in time and the universe.

I am so lucky that my Emma's recollection is so sharp concerning the curious events which brought me here a little over seven years ago. Between my earliest journal entries and her accurate memories, I have a vague idea of my life in another century.

But I can't imagine giving up what I have here for a chance to see flying ships, typewriters that think for themselves, or men walking on the moon.

I can't envision these things because I can't imagine a life without Emma. I have no trouble believing that she was the sole reason I traveled through a century of time. She is the love of my lifetime, of a hundred life-times.

Our sons are very much our life, our purpose, our joy, and the source of occasional consternation. They grow bigger and stronger each year, constantly surprising us with their intelligence and ingenuity. We miss having Ford around, he being the one most capable of corralling them when their enthusiasms grow beyond bounds, but we understand the rigors of college life. I just hope Timothy and Nicholas and the baby to come take to education as well as their Uncle Ford has.

The day grows stronger and my shift starts soon. Margin has grown over the past years, surviving the silver bust in '93 by producing a healthy vein of copper which is keeping the town afloat. Both my duties as sheriff and Emma's as doctor have grown with the increase in population.

It is time to leave the nineteenth century behind and look toward the future. I can think of no better place than Margin and no better companion than my wife Emma with whom to share this glorious new century.

John Barrett Callaghan

Dear Reader,

The story of Barrett, Emma, Harvey and Johnny sprang from a variety of shadowy places in my mind. But perhaps, most importantly, there's the lasting effect that television and movie interpretations of time travel have made on me. I've gone back with Spock and Kirk (Not Harvey!) and the crew to rescue whales, I've leaped with Sam and Al and I've watched Doc Brown build a complicated machine to generate a single dirty-looking ice cube. And what about love in another place and time? I'm astounded at how true love changed Doc Brown in a hero when found his Clara. I was captivated by H.G. Wells, watching him fall in love with a woman of the future and battle Jack the Ripper for her life. I was mesmerized by Christopher Reeve as he traveled back Somewhere In Time to be with the woman he loved.

And typically, an author brings some sort of personal experience to every story. In my case, I share with Barrett the same moments of encompassing, debilitating fear when I first went underground. The first few minutes of gut-wrenching, throat-closing fear I experienced when I first entered the Mulga Coal Mine in Alabama will stay with me forever. But I survived and still have my hard hat and some good stories that can't be shared in polite company.

Time flies, time will tell, the times they are a-changing. We've always been preoccupied with time in one way or the other. I hope you'll have time to come along for the ride the next time I visit Margin.

Laura

(or take time to write.)
P.O. Box 10922
Burke, VA 22009